Barren Lives

THE TEXAS PAN-AMERICAN SERIES

University of Texas Press, Austin

Barren Lives

(VIDAS SÊCAS)

by GRACILIANO RAMOS

Translated with an Introduction by
Ralph Edward Dimmick

ILLUSTRATED BY CHARLES UMLAUF

The Texas Pan American Series is published with the assistance
of a revolving publication fund established by the Pan American
Sulphur Company and other friends of Latin America in Texas.
Publication of this book was also assisted by a grant from the
Rockefeller Foundation through the Latin American Translation
program of the Association of American University Presses.

International Standard Book Number 0-292-70133-0
Library of Congress Catalog Card Number 65-16468
Copyright © 1965 by Heloisa de Medeiros Ramos
Printed in the United States of America

Seventh paperback printing, 1992

The paper used in this publication meets the minimum
requirements of American National Standard for Information
Sciences—Permanence of Paper for Printed Library Materials,
ANSI Z39.48-1984.

INTRODUCTION

The governor of Alagoas—a small, backwater state on the bulge of Brazil—could hardly believe his eyes. There among the municipal reports for the year 1928, dismal bureaucratic documents in which the accomplishments of local administrators were exaggerated with bombast or their inaction disguised by a cloud of obfuscating clichés, was one the like of which had never crossed his desk before. Wrote the mayor of Palmeira dos Índios: "I do not know whether the municipal administration is good or bad. Perhaps it could be worse. . . . I must have made numerous foolish mistakes, all attributable to my limited intelligence." The style, simple and direct, often wryly humorous, was as refreshing as the author's modesty and candor. At times it took on the raciness of popular speech: the mayor could see no point to wasting money on a telegram of condolence just because a deputy in the assembly had "kicked the bucket."

In Brazil there has never been that divorce between intellectuals and government which is so often deplored in the United States—as the mayor of Palmeira dos Índios was to write on a later occasion, "Artists as a rule escape from hunger by getting government jobs"—and his municipal report for 1928 was soon brought to the attention of literary circles throughout the country. Augusto Frederico Schmidt, an unlikely combination of romantic poet and successful businessman, who at the time had fused his interests in a publishing venture, sensed, as he said, that the mayor must have the manuscript of a novel hidden away in a drawer someplace, and offered his services to the writer. The guess proved correct, and the publisher's offer was accepted, but not until 1933, owing to the economic and political disturbances of the intervening years, did the book appear: *Caetés,* by Graciliano Ramos.

In the galaxy of new writers whose emergence in the early 1930's made those years one of the most exciting periods in the history of Brazilian letters, Graciliano Ramos was a relative oldster. He had been born in 1892 in the little town of Quebrângulo, in rural Alagoas, but while still an infant had been taken to his maternal grandfather's ranch near Buíque, in the neighboring state of Pernambuco. This is range country, too dry for crops, subject to periodic droughts which bring death to cattle and ruin to the owners. This was the region of Ramos' earliest recollections, and this is the background of *Barren Lives.*

Ramos' childhood is brilliantly evoked in a volume of memoirs entitled *Infância.* He presents his father, "a grave man with a broad forehead—one of the handsomest I ever saw—sound teeth, a firm-set jaw, and a frightening voice"; his mother, "a puny, aggressive, bad-tempered matron, always bustling about, with a knobby head ill covered by thin hair, an evil-looking mouth, and evil-looking eyes, which, in moments of wrath, gleamed with a flame of madness"; his two grandfathers, one a bankrupt plantation owner, from whom "perhaps I inherited my absurd vocation for useless things," the other "a man of immense vitality, resistant to drought, first prosperous, then all but ruined, courageously rebuilding his fortune"; and a host of other figures, some of whom, such as the ranch hand José Baía, appear without so much as a change of name in Ramos' novel *Anguish.*

As is perhaps suggested by the description of his parents, Ramos' early years were not happy ones. His mother had little time for him: the chapter of *Barren Lives* concerned with the older boy is a reminiscence of the author's childhood. His father, in the patriarchal tradition of Brazilian society, was the incarnation of authority, at times mercilessly blind. Graciliano's first encounter with "justice" was a paternal whiplashing occasioned by the disappearance of a belt—a beating for which the father made no amends even when he discovered that the boy was in no way responsible. Viewing his father's actions with half a century's perspective, Ramos found his outbursts understandable. Unlike his indomitable father-in-law, the elder Ramos gave way before the ravages of drought, abandoning ranching for a series of ill-starred ventures as a shopkeeper, first in Buíque, later in Viçosa and Palmeira dos Índios, back in the state of Alagoas. Unsure of his position, forced to scrape before his creditors and the local political bosses, he vented his spleen on his debtors, his social inferiors, and his children.

He made at least one significant contribution to his son's education, however. Ramos' account of his early schooling is a depressing one: cruel discipline, rote learning, incompetent teachers, classroom material totally inappropriate to the juvenile mind. At the age of seven, a lad with no knowledge of Portuguese beyond the rudimentary vocabulary used by the inhabitants of the backlands was assigned to read the *Lusiads!* Small wonder that two years later he was still "all but illiterate." Then one evening, counter to all custom, Graciliano's father called him to fetch a book and read. The book was an adventure story, telling of a family lost in the woods on a winter's night, pursued by wolves. Under his father's questioning, and with his translations into "kitchen language" of the more high-flown literary expressions, Graciliano's understanding unfolded and his curiosity was whetted. The father's tutoring lasted only three nights, but the boy's interest in books, once aroused, was to accompany him to the end of his life.

This interest was of prime importance for his educational development. While at the age of twelve he was sent to secondary school in the state capital, Maceió, he never completed the course, and such culture as he acquired resulted almost entirely from his own independent readings. The Ramos household seems to have numbered few books among its possessions, but the notary of Viçosa had a library, and from him Graciliano borrowed his first work of literary value, *O Guarani* ("The Guarani Indian"), by José de Alencar, the Brazilian counterpart of James Fenimore Cooper. The postmaster was another source of supply. A man of literary pretensions himself, he encouraged Graciliano to write for a small sheet he had founded, and the resulting products appeared there, much embellished by the boy's mentor. Local stocks proving insufficient for his appetite, however, Graciliano took to filching coins from the cash drawer in his father's shop, so that he might order the works that so tempted him in publishers' catalogs received from Rio. "These crimes caused me no remorse," he declared, saying that he managed to convince himself of his father's tacit approval of his conduct. And indeed the elder Ramos must have had some idea of the origin of the volumes that accumulated on his son's bookshelf.

One is not surprised to learn that the adolescent reader's taste ran to the novels of Zola and his Portuguese contemporary Eça de Queiroz, then at the apogee of their fame, and the appeal offered by Balzac is understandable. One is surprised, however, to discover that translations of Dostoevsky and Gorki had made their way to the backlands of Brazil in the first decade of our century, and that they were avidly devoured by the young Graciliano.

The years of Ramos' early manhood are a somewhat obscure period in his life. In 1914 he went to Rio to try his hand at journalism. Unprepossessing in appearance, without influential friends, he failed to make his way there, and 1915 found him back in Palmeira dos Índios, where he married. To support himself and his family, he turned, like his father, to shopkeeping. His literary urgings were satisfied by occasional contributions to short-lived local periodicals and, beginning in 1926, by work upon a novel. The novel was not finished till 1928, the year of his election as mayor. By this time he was married for the second time, his first wife having died after but five years of wedded life.

The literary consequence of his venture into politics has already been noted. Once launched as a writer, with the publication of *Caetés* in 1933, he brought out three other novels in rather rapid succession: *São Bernardo*, in 1934; *Anguish*, in 1936; and *Barren Lives*, in 1938.

Meanwhile his material existence had undergone radical changes. The reports of his two years as mayor of Palmeira dos Índios so impressed the governor of Alagoas that, early in 1930, he invited Ramos to Maceió to assume the direction of the state press. He remained in this position until the end of 1931, having strangely survived the Vargas revolution, which toppled his patron along with other governors. A return to Palmeira dos Índios, where he briefly established a school, and a long sojourn in the hospital marked 1932. In 1933 the man who had never completed secondary school was appointed state director of public instruction. With the same practical objectivity and single-minded adherence to conviction that had characterized him as a municipal administrator, he undertook the reform of teaching in Alagoas. It was not surprising that his innovations won him enemies, both overt and covert, among those whose interests were unfavorably affected.

Whether or not those enemies were responsible for his dismissal and imprisonment in 1936 is, however, open to question. The frustrated revolt of the National Liberal Alliance at the end of 1935 led to wholesale arrests and deportations. Ramos, with countless others from all walks of life, was crammed into the hold of a coastal vessel and shipped to Rio, where he was first sent to a penitentiary, then to a prison camp on an island off the coast, and finally back again to the penitentiary. His health, precarious since his hospital experience of 1932, was definitely ruined by the hardships to which he was thus exposed, and his last two months of incarceration were spent in the prison infirmary.

No formal charges were ever brought against him: he was released with no more explanation than had been given for his

arrest. This Kafka-like experience is related at length and in
searing detail in a work with which Ramos was occupied at the
time of his death, *Memórias do Cárcere* ("Prison Memoirs"). A
curious air of resignation pervades the book: there are no out-
cries at injustice or official barbarity, no attacks on the political
order, no attempts at self-justification. Although he admits that
his offspring had gone about painting leftist slogans in public
places, he himself did not officially adhere to the Communist
Party until 1945. Even then his act seems to have been one of
protest against the established order rather than a statement of
Marxist conviction.

In any case, whatever the grounds for his imprisonment may
have been, it was only a little more than a year after his release
that he was offered and accepted appointment as a federal in-
spector of education in Vargas' fascistic New State. With the
salary from this post and the income from his books and periodi-
cal articles, Ramos eked out an existence until his death in 1953.
He did not return to Alagoas, but instead took up residence in
Rio, where he enjoyed great respect in literary circles. Elected
president of the Brazilian Writers' Union, he made a trip in this
capacity to Czechoslovakia and the Soviet Union in 1952 to attend a literary congress in Moscow.

Ramos' reputation rests upon his last three novels and the two
autobiographical works which have been mentioned. Besides
these his other writings are of relatively little interest, save for
the light they occasionally throw on aspects of his character or
literary processes. Thus *Viagem* ("Journey"), unfinished at his
death, in which his European experiences are related in routine
fashion, reveals an attitude of little more than open-minded neu-

trality toward life behind the Iron Curtain. One might have expected more enthusiasm from a declared—even if nominal—Communist. *Linhas Tortas* ("Crooked Lines") and *Viventes das Alagoas* ("People of Alagoas"), posthumous collections of his contributions to periodicals, contain views of the author on writing, writers, and the Brazilian temperament. Ramos thrice tried his hand at children's literature: with a collection of tall tales, *Histórias de Alexandre* ("Stories Told by Alexander"); with an insipid short narrative, which nonetheless won a prize from the Ministry of Education, *A Terra dos Meninos Pelados* ("The Land of Hairless Children"); and with a *Pequena História da República* ("Short History of the Republic"). The last-mentioned was Ramos' entry in a contest for school textbooks. It is difficult to conceive how he could have expected any regime, least of all one of the type prevailing in 1942, to accept so irreverent a treatment of the nation's history, or how he could have supposed juvenile readers would appreciate the irony which makes his account of public figures and events wryly diverting to adults. Finally, he wrote a collection of short stories, published first as *Dois Dedos* ("Two Fingers"), and later, in augmented form, as *Insônia* ("Insomnia"). Of these something will be said in connection with *Barren Lives*.

Ramos seems to have regretted the publication of *Caetés*. One day during his imprisonment he observed, "with a shudder of revulsion," that one of his fellow inmates was engaged in reading the novel and begged, "For heaven's sake, don't read that! It's trash."

Ramos' judgment is overly harsh. While not worthy to stand beside his later novels, *Caetés* is nevertheless a very respectable example of the masterwork of an apprentice—the proof that he has absorbed the lesson of his elders and is ready to strike out on his own. It falls clearly within the current of post-Naturalism, showing great concern with the establishment of a milieu in all its details, dwelling on events of the most ordinary nature, presenting a slice of life in small-town northeastern Brazil. The chief influence to be noted is that of Eça de Queiroz, whose use of a similar device in his *A Ilustre Casa de Ramires* ("The Illustrious House of Ramires") may have inspired Ramos to assign the writing of a historical novel as a pastime for his protagonist-narrator, João Valério. This undertaking, concerned with the Caeté Indians who once inhabited Alagoas—and whose chief recorded exploit seems to have been the cannibalizing of the first bishop of Brazil—not only provides the title of the novel but also gives rise to passages in which Ramos reveals something of his approach to the literary process. Here João Valério has been trying to describe the shipwreck which caused the ill-starred bishop to fall into the hands—and stomachs—of the savages:

With a hesitant pen I meditated a long while on the floating wreckage. I had counted on that shipwreck; I had imagined an impressive description full of vivid adjectives. And there I had only a colorless, insignificant account of a second-rate disaster. It was short too: written in a large hand, and with some words crossed out, it ran to only eighteen lines. Putting a sinking ship in my book—what foolishness! When had I ever seen a galleon? Besides it may have been a caravel. Or a barkentine.

Like João Valério, Ramos, from the beginning, found himself incapable not only of high-flown language but of drawing episodes out beyond the essential. He was also incapable, or felt himself to be so, of describing that with which he did not have firsthand experience.

The plot of *Caetés* is a simple one. João Valério, a store clerk, nourishes an adulterous desire for Luísa, his employer's wife. She yields to him during an absence of her husband. The latter, informed of her infidelity, commits suicide. Though now free to marry, João Valério and Luísa go their separate ways, their passion dead.

About these central figures revolves a host of minor ones—politicians, boardinghouse keepers, clergy, merchants—occupied with the petty intrigues and gossip of small-town existence. They are singularly lifelike. A number of Ramos' acquaintances claimed to recognize their portraits and accused him of writing a *roman à clef*, a charge that greatly annoyed him. He himself says, regarding the genesis of his characters, "One thing surprised me: my personages began to talk. Previously my wretched, abandoned, incomplete creatures had been all but mute, perhaps because they had tried to express themselves in an overly correct Portuguese, altogether impossible in Brazil. My book turned out to be full of dialog; it reads like a play."

Indeed, it is largely through dialog that the characters reveal themselves, bit by bit. The resulting psychological portraits are doubtless superficial, for people are not wont to bare their souls in casual dinner-table conversations. The abundant dialog also offers another advantage: by its liveliness it causes the reader to all but overlook the paucity of narrative element.

In *Caetés*, as in his later novels, Ramos is concerned much less with telling a story than with studying an individual in a particular situation. The critic Antônio Cândido penetratingly observes: "Without recourse to introspection, inner life is described through the *situation* of a character within a context of actions and events. A double perspective results, for, if the character is revealed by the events, these present themselves in the light of the problems affecting him." Ramos' preoccupation with the case of the individual, with his particular view of ambient reality, is emphasized by the fact that each of his first three novels is related by the protagonist, an arrangement which of necessity results in subordinating all events and characters to his private angle of vision. (Indeed, save for the short stories and *Barren Lives*, virtually the whole of Ramos' writing is in the first person, the author speaking either directly for himself, as in the case of the autobiographical works, or through the mouth of a fictional creation.)

Although not only this approach to the novel but also a number of Ramos' other characteristics—the spareness and precision of his vocabulary, the brevity of his periods, his disillusioned view of life, his wry humor—are to be found in *Caetés*, that book by no means prepares the reader for the novels that were to follow, all of which show a mastery of style and technique that assign Graciliano Ramos a place apart in Brazilian letters. They are remarkably different one from another, and each has found critics to support it as the author's masterpiece.

"Stark" is perhaps the adjective which best befits *São Bernardo*, by reason of the obduracy of the protagonist, the harshness of the book's atmosphere, the bareness of the narrative, and the strength of the work as a literary creation.

If in *Caetés* Ramos described the society surrounding him in

Palmeira dos Índios, for *São Bernardo* he went back to an earlier period in his existence, situating the action in the district of Viçosa. This was a region of both farmers and stock raisers, whose mutually repellent interests led to what at one time was said to be the highest homicide rate in any municipality in Brazil. Small property owners, particularly crop raisers, were systematically eliminated—with a rifle or through economic and political pressure—by the larger proprietors, usually cattlemen. Only the strongest and most ruthless survived.

The story Ramos tells is well suited to so harsh a background. The protagonist-narrator, Paulo Honório, is a self-made man. A foundling, he has forged ahead in life by hook, by crook, by indomitable will, and by endless energy. At the age of forty-five he has achieved the goal of his existence: he is the owner of the property which gives the book its name, a rural estate on which he had once been a field laborer; the ne'er-do-well son of the former proprietor is now in his employ. With a view to begetting an heir, he takes a wife, Madalena, a woman of great goodness and compassion for all. Her charity and sensitivity are totally incompatible with Paulo Honório's brutal, possessive nature. He cannot conceive of Madalena as other than an item of his property, and she, weary of an unending struggle against cruelty, misunderstanding, and jealousy, commits suicide. Paulo Honório realizes at last that he had, in his own way, truly loved his wife, that everything else has no real meaning for him. To fill the empty hours, to unburden the soul he had been unable to reveal even to Madalena, he undertakes to set their story down on paper.

Unlike the protagonist of *Caetés,* Paulo Honório is not a function of his environment; on the contrary the environment is entirely subordinated to his own compelling personality. Paulo Honório embodies the instinct of ownership. It is not a question of avarice; for Paulo Honório all humanity is divided into two classes—men of property and those who work for them. All his efforts have been bent to achieving entrance into the former class. The consequences of his single-mindedness he recognizes in a final summing up:

I do not think I was always selfish and brutal. My calling made me so. . . . This way of life destroyed me. I am a cripple. I must have a very small heart, blank spots in my brain, nerves different from those of other men.

Hypertrophied though he may be, he is not, however, all of a piece. He still possesses human feelings, and it is the inner conflict to which they give rise that makes of him a dramatic personality, that leaves him in the end not one of life's victors but one of life's vanquished.

It would be difficult to imagine a work more thoroughly reduced to essentials than *São Bernardo*. Paulo Honório's early career is related in a dozen short, but extraordinarily vivid, paragraphs. There is not a single description for its own sake. The phrases that evoke the property of São Bernardo are of the briefest and are always introduced to further in some way the development of events. Here, for example, is the opening of the scene in which Paulo Honório proposes to take over the estate from Luís Padilha, the ne'er-do-well into whose hands it has fallen by inheritance:

I rode toward the plantation house, which looked even older and in worse need of repair under the pouring rain. The spiderflowers had not been cut. I jumped off the horse and walked in, stamping my feet, my spurs clinking. Luís Padilha was asleep in the main room, stretched out in a filthy hammock, oblivious to the rain that beat at the windows and the leaks from the roof which were flooding the floor.

Everything needed to explain Padilha's subsequent acquiescence is here suggested to the reader—his indolence, the neglect into which he has let his property fall, the domineering manner in which Paulo Honório approaches him, stamping, and entering without so much as a by-your-leave.

While the conversations are fully as natural as those of *Caetés*, Ramos has limited them, like all else, to the significant. The sharpness of the interchanges gives them often an air of verbal duels between the characters.

Ramos, speaking through his protagonist-narrator, describes the reduction to essentials quite simply: "The process I have adopted is this: I extract a few elements from an event, and reject the rest as waste."

Stylistically, *São Bernardo* is a tour de force. The short, abrupt sentences, with their energetic vocabulary, are thoroughly expressive of the personality of the narrator. The writing has the ease and naturalness of popular speech, without recourse to dialect, looseness of construction, imprecision in choice of words, or syntactical error.

It would be hard to conceive of a work more different in overall effect from *São Bernardo* than the novel which followed, *Angústia* (translated as *Anguish* by L. C. Kaplan, New York,

1946). Once again the story is told in retrospect by the protagonist, but whereas Paulo Honório is a man strong of body and purpose, who has battled his way from field laborer to landed proprietor, the Luís da Silva of *Anguish* is the abulic final offshoot of a decadent family of plantation owners, reduced to a meager existence as a petty clerk in a government office. While *São Bernardo* has an out-of-doors atmosphere of space and light, the drama of *Anguish* unfolds in the dark, tortuous recesses of the protagonist's mind. Dialog, so brilliantly handled in the preceding novels, is abandoned for an all-but-uninterrupted inner monolog. Straightforward narrative is replaced by a fragmented confession, in which events are presented in a complex interplay of objective reality, memory, and speculation. The view of persons and events is not merely one-sided; it is deformed by the distorted vision of the protagonist.

The new manner is suggested by this passage from the beginning of the novel:

If I could, I would give up everything and resume my travels. This monotonous existence, chained to a desk from nine to twelve and from two to five, is stupefying. I might as well be a clam. Stupefying. When they close the office, I drag myself over to the clock tower and take the first streetcar to Land's End.

What can Marina be doing? I try to get her out of my mind. I could take a trip, get drunk, commit suicide.

I can see my dead body, thin as a rail, my teeth showing in a grin, my eyes like a pair of peeled grapes, my hands with their tobacco-stained fingers crossed on my hollow chest. . . .

I shake off these depressing thoughts. They come and go shamelessly, and with them the recollection of Julião Tavares. Unbearable.

I try to get my mind off these things. I'm not a rat, I don't want to be a rat. I seek distraction looking at the street. . . .

Fifteen years ago it was different. You couldn't hear the church bell for the noise of the streetcars. My room, on the second floor, was as hot as hell. So at the hour the other boarders were leaving for medical school, I would go over to the public park and read the crime reports in the shade of the trees. Of course the boardinghouse has been closed and Miss Aurora, who was old even then, has died.

If Paulo Honório personifies the instinct of ownership, Luís da Silva is the embodiment of frustration. The thought of his family reminds him how far he has come down in the world; his bureaucratic routine gives him no sense of purpose in life; an overdeveloped critical faculty makes him keenly aware not only of the lack of merit of those more favored by fortune but also of his own shortcomings. He had once written a collection of poems; unable to pay for their publication under his own name, he has sold them one by one to others who wished to figure as possessors of literary talents.

Timid in his personal relations, particularly with women ("sex for me was always something painful, complicated, and incomplete"), he is ensnared into an engagement by Marina, the idle daughter of a neighbor family. She spends on a trousseau what he has saved and borrowed for household goods. At this point a man appears who is the exact opposite of Luís de Silva. Julião Tavares, the son of a merchant, has money, social position, women, self-confidence, and an untroubled conscience. Taking a passing fancy to Marina, he seduces and abandons her. All of Luís' pent-up frustration finds its object in his triumphant rival. So obsessed with him does he become that at last he is led to action. One night, as Julião returns from a visit to his latest conquest, Luís strangles him. He tells his story upon recovery from the extended period of nervous prostration that ensued.

Though attention centers on the personality of Luís da Silva, the novel offers a varied gallery of vivid portraits. Particularly striking is the servant woman Vitória, who buries her savings in the back yard only to dig them up for constant recounting, and who is deeply perturbed when, without her knowledge, Luís borrows from the hoard and makes restitution in coins of different denomination.

Despite the nightmare air of the book, many of the characters are drawn from life. Luís da Silva's grandfather, for example, is patterned on Ramos' own; the latter's henchman José Baía appears under his own name. The original of Moisés, the Jewish revolutionary, was a source of concern to Ramos at the time of his incarceration.

It is curious that this somber story, with its prison-like atmosphere, should have appeared precisely at that darkest period in the author's life—curious because no relation of cause and effect exists between the two facts. The book had been finished prior to Ramos' arrest; one of his many worries in jail was how it might fare in the hands of the publisher. Persecution of the author did, however, contribute to the success with which the novel met on its appearance. It was greeted as a masterpiece; the author was hailed as a Brazilian Dostoevsky. Somewhat more reserved views are expressed today. Antônio Cândido, while paying due tribute to *Anguish* as a tour de force, finds it "overdone." The work is still, however, the one regarded by a majority of critics as Ramos' best.

The genesis of his next and final novel, *Barren Lives,* Graciliano Ramos describes thus:

In 1937 I wrote some lines on the death of a dog, an animal that turned out overly intelligent to my way of thinking, and for this reason somewhat different from my bipeds. Afterwards I did a few pages on the dog's owners. These pieces were sold, one by one, to newspapers and magazines. When [the publisher] José Olímpio asked me for a book at the beginning of last year, I invented a few more narratives which could just as easily be short stories as chapters of a novel. Thus there came into being Fabiano, his wife, their two boys, and the dog, the last creatures I have put in circulation.

It is interesting to note that all of Ramos' novels, by his own account, began as short stories. *São Bernardo* and *Anguish* were sketched in embryonic form before he took up the theme of *Caetés*; in this last case "the short story grew all too long and deteriorated into a novel." *Caetés* having been accepted for publication, Ramos returned to his earlier sketches, developing them too into novels.

Barren Lives is a compromise between genres. The book possesses unity: it presents a cycle in the life of a herdsman and his family, from their arrival at a ranch as refugees from one drought to their departure in flight from another. Yet the individual chapters are relatively independent entities; their order could be altered in various ways without detriment to the whole. Not only were the first parts written for separate publication as short stories, but Ramos himself included three chapters ("Jail," "Feast Day," "The Dog") with other selected short narratives in a volume he published in 1946 under the title of *Histórias Incompletas* ("Incomplete Stories").

xxiv

The title, as Antônio Cândido shrewdly notes, is perhaps more significant than Ramos intended, for it well indicates the deficiency that marks his work as a short story writer. None of his compositions in this genre forms a satisfying narrative unit. Each seems but a sketch for, or fragment of, a larger work. In *Barren Lives*, however, the recurrence of the same figures in varying situations gradually produces that sense of wholeness requisite to the self-sufficiency of a work of art.

Of all his output, *Barren Lives* is the work in which Ramos is most concerned with narration, with telling a story, tenuous though it may be. As in the case of his short stories, he here abandons the use of the first person for the third. This technique does not result in any sense of detachment, however, for he still writes at all times from the viewpoint of one of the characters. Five of the chapters in fact are named for the personage whose vision of events colors their presentation. In four more Fabiano reappears as the dominant figure. In the remaining chapters the viewpoint shifts from character to character. Only in the closing sentence of the books does Ramos, perhaps regrettably, speak from a standpoint foreign to his characters.

One can hardly speak of psychological analysis in the case of Fabiano and his family; they are not so much simple as elementary. Their actions are guided by instinct rather than thought; Fabiano's attempt to understand how he comes to be in jail, for instance, suggests that ratiocination is beyond his capabilities. Ramos can therefore treat the dog on very much the same level as her masters, as a member of the family.

Dialog, of which Ramos had made such skillful use in earlier works, is here almost totally missing. Having a minimum of ideas to convey to one another, the members of the family are generally silent, to such an extent that the parrot they once owned never learned to talk. A gesture or an interjection serves for a large part of the communication among them.

The personages of *Barren Lives* are admirably studied in regard to their surroundings. This is, in fact, of all Ramos' works the one in which the relation between man and his milieu is most clearly developed. In *Caetés* the characters are distinctly small-town products, but the town might have been any one of countless others in Brazil rather than Palmeira dos Índios. The action of *São Bernardo* is set in the district of Viçosa and that of *Anguish* presumably in Maceió, but the locale is of little importance to the development of personalities and events.

Barren Lives, however, could take place nowhere save in the drought-ridden interior of northeastern Brazil. (The literal meaning of the Portuguese title, *Vidas Sêcas*, "Dry Lives," reflects both the parched atmosphere of the region and the desiccating effect it has on the existence of its inhabitants.) It is the work which identifies Ramos with the so-called novel of the Northeast, one of the most fertile veins in Brazilian literature since 1930. Its practitioners have dealt with varying aspects of the region—José Lins do Rêgo with the sugar plantations of coastal Pernambuco and Paraíba, Jorge Amado with the street urchins of Salvador and the cacao wars of southern Bahia, for example. No aspect of the area has attracted greater attention, doubtless by reason of the dramatic effects it offers, than the terrible droughts that periodically visit the backlands. Only a hardy breed could survive such trials, especially when prospects of reward are so few.

Fabiano and his family own little more than the clothes on their backs. Their few belongings are easily contained in a tin trunk which Vitória balances on her head when they set off on one of their forced treks. Their pleasures are small ones—an occasional swig of rum for Fabiano, a pair of high-heeled shoes for Vitória, a trip to town for all at the time of the Christmas festivities. Fabiano is a good herdsman, and the ranch propers under his management as long as the rains come. He gets no thanks from the proprietor, however, whose conversation with his employee usually takes the form of a dressing-down. By a skillful system of advances of money and overcharges for interest, the proprietor sees, moreover, that little or nothing in the form of wages comes into Fabiano's hands at the end of the year. Tradesmen cheat the ranch hand, townspeople scorn him as a bumpkin, a policeman avenges his ill luck at cards by throwing him into jail. Yet Fabiano accepts all this abuse as his natural lot; so was his father used before him, and he has only vague illusions that his sons may know a better life. The height of his wife's ambition is ownership of a single piece of furniture, a comfortable bed.

It is to be remarked that Ramos has no recourse to the more dramatic aspects of life in the backlands—banditry and religious fanaticism—which crop up frequently in other novels of the region. His very descriptions of the drought are sober; he suggests by details, such as the vultures circling in to peck out the eyes of moribund animals, in preference to painting a large-scale picture of natural catastrophe. One might recall in this regard João Valério, whose attempt at a grandiose depiction of shipwreck resulted in a "colorless, insignificant account of a second-rate disaster." Unlike João Valério, who had never seen a galleon, Graciliano Ramos had experienced drought from his earliest years. The restraint of his treatment reflects his austere temperament rather than any insufficiency of knowledge.

It is difficult to say why Ramos to all intents and purposes turned his back on fiction after the publication of *Barren Lives*. Perhaps he felt he had exhausted the varieties of approach open to a writer of his particular abilities and preferred to avoid any air of repeating himself. Again it may have been a desire to comment still more directly upon the world of his experience that led him to abandon fictional mouthpieces and to devote the major literary efforts of his last years to autobiography.

Infância ("Childhood"), in its poetic presentation of distant figures and events, preserves something of the atmosphere of fiction. Ramos in a sense was still writing from a viewpoint external to himself—that of the boy he had been half a century earlier, a boy who had left a few traces of his existence in *Anguish* and *Barren Lives*. The distinguished critic Álvaro Lins holds "Childhood" to be the best-written of all Ramos' works, and indeed it is one of great distinction and charm. It possesses full literary autonomy; while of much interest for the light it throws on the man and his fictional compositions, it can be read and enjoyed for itself alone, as a story or collection of stories.

The "Prison Memoirs," on the other hand, constitute a spiritual diary of a period much nearer at hand, which had left an indelible impression on Ramos' mind. One cannot but wonder at the wealth of its recorded detail, even if, as the author admits, it may not be accurate in all particulars, for it is in its entirety a reconstruction from memory. (Ramos took extended notes during the first part of his imprisonment, but these were later lost.)

Highly uneven—pedestrian passages being interspersed with pages of great power—the "Memoirs" would undoubtedly have benefited from tightening and revision had not death overtaken the author as he was approaching the end of his chronicle.

Ramos once wrote that in his view the principal deficiency from which Brazilian fiction of his day suffered was "lack of careful observation of the facts that are to enter into the composition of the work of art," adding that, "in an undertaking so complex as the novel, ignorance of those facts is detrimental to characterization and results in a lack of verisimilitude in the narrative." He himself was constant in writing only of that with which he had firsthand acquaintance and a feeling of intimacy. In an interview given a year before his death he declared:

I could never conceive an abstract novel, a work of escape literature. My novels are all concerned with the Northeast, because it was there that I spent my youth; it is what I really know and feel. I have lived in Rio for twenty years [sic], but I could never succeed in writing a novel about Rio, because I do not know the city.

Ramos did not, however, feel any scruple about rearranging facts to suit artistic purpose. In *São Bernardo,* Paulo Honório describes the process which we may assume was Ramos' own:

This conversation, obviously, did not proceed exactly as I have set it down on paper. There were pauses, repetitions, misunderstandings, and contradictions, all quite natural when people speak without thinking of the record. I reproduce what I consider interesting. I suppressed a number of passages and altered others. . . . For example, when I dragged Costa Brito over to the clock, I told him what I thought of him in four or five indecent terms. This abuse, unnecessary since it neither added to nor detracted from the effect of the whiplashes I gave him, has gone by the board as you will note if you reread the scene of the attack. That scene, expurgated of obscenities, is described with relative sobriety.

Sobriety is indeed one of the key characteristics of Ramos' manner. It has been noted in the discussion of *Barren Lives*, for example, that the author avoids the more melodramatic aspects of life in the backlands and that in picturing the catastrophic effects of the drought he exercises great restraint. Even Luís da Silva's murder of Julião Tavares, the most violent scene in all Ramos' writing, admirable as a revelation of the workings of the narrator's tortured mind, is related with great simplicity of terms.

Ramos' constant aim was to obtain maximum effect from minimum resources. What he has to say he says in relatively few words. Save for the "Prison Memoirs," none of his works can be described as long. As novels, *São Bernardo* and *Barren Lives* are decidedly short. Ramos' sentences too are for the most part brief; at times they seem almost curt. Descriptive adjectives and adverbs are held to a minimum: a sample six-page chapter of *São Bernardo* exhibits but two of the latter and two dozen of the former.

Ramos was greatly concerned with what he considered acceptable standards of literary expression. Up to the third decade of the present century, Brazilian authors tended to take the usage of Portugal as their model, without regard for the transformations which time, geographical separation, and the introduction of new ethnic elements had of necessity wrought in Portuguese as spoken in Brazil. The Modernist movement of the 1920's revolted against this practice of "speaking one language and writing another," and advocated vernacular usage as the basis of literary style. The inevitable question, of course, was what level of usage was to be taken as standard. If turns of popular speech often brought savoriness and spontaneity to literature, excessive reliance on the model provided by the man in the street, or in the field, resulted in what Ramos characterized as "the intentional mistakes of certain citizens who systematically write things the wrong way." Such writers, he continued, "are purists who have gone astray, seeking to create an artificial language of halting effect." Recognizing, on the other hand, that an "overly correct Portuguese" was "altogether impossible in Brazil," he sought to steer a middle course, avoiding both the stilted and the incorrect. He succeeded admirably. One might well apply to Ramos what he said of one of his contemporaries: "He expresses himself correctly and without floweriness; this gives his prose an air of naturalness which deceives the unwary reader. We do not perceive the artifice; we have the impression that the effect is altogether spontaneous, obtained without effort of any kind."

Álvaro Lins, for his part, describes Ramos' style thus:

Graciliano Ramos' prose is modern by reason of its leanness, the vocabulary it employs, and the taste it exhibits in the use of words and syntactical constructions. It is classic in its correctness and in the tone of what one might term Biblical dignity that marks the sentences. Its distinction derives not from sensual beauty but from precision—from a capacity for transmitting sensations and impressions with a minimum of metaphors and images, simply through the skillful interplay of words.

Both for the transparency of his writing and for the pessimistic view he takes of life, Ramos has been compared to the greatest of his Brazilian predecessors, Machado de Assis. The aristocratically disillusioned prose of the latter, most often manifested in ironic wit, contrasts with a more profoundly fatalistic attitude on the part of Ramos. It is well exemplified by the passage setting forth Fabiano's feelings following his settling of accounts with the ranch owner:

Couldn't they see he was a man of flesh and blood? It was his duty to work for others, naturally. He knew his place. That was all right. He was born to this lot; it was nobody's fault that it was a hard one. What could he do? Could he change fate? If anyone were to tell him it was possible to better one's lot, he would be amazed. He had come into the world to break untamed horses, cure cattle ailments by prayer, and fix fences from winter to summer. It was fate. His father had lived like that, his grandfather too. . . . He accepted the situation; he did not ask for more. If only they gave him what was coming to him, it was all right. But they didn't. He was a poor devil; like a dog, all he got was bones. Why then did rich people go and take part of the bones?

Life is essentially unjust, and there is nothing anyone can do about it: this is Ramos' view. Other writers of his generation, particularly those from his own Northeast, likewise saw the injustice; they, however, felt that something could and should be done about it. Several took an active part in left-wing politics, and in their works there breathes a conviction that sooner or later a new day must dawn for the disinherited of the earth. Not so Ramos. He admitted of changes in individual situations: a Paulo Honório could rise, a Luís Padilha could sink. There will always, however, be oppressed and oppressors. Toward both he took an equally cold, one might say clinical, attitude. Suffering he treats with dignity but without compassion.

Though Ramos seems to have taken human pettiness and meanness for granted, human generosity caused him surprise. Gratuitous acts of kindness of which he was the object during prison days were a source of unresolved wonder to him. Is it coincidence that the work which followed upon that period of his existence was not the somber *Anguish* but *Barren Lives*, relatively speaking the most optimistic—or perhaps one should say least pessimistic—of his creations? Despite the natural disasters and human injustices which overtake them, Fabiano and his family breathe an elemental heroism; they bear witness to the unconquerable spirit that bids man carry on, whatever adversity he may be called to face.

By reason of the keenness of his psychological insight, of his deep feeling for the vernacular, of his unfailing sense of proportion, of his skilled craftsmanship in construction, Ramos has been able to fashion from the simplest and most unpromising of materials works which stand among the most impressive creations of modern Brazilian literature. Commonplace incidents, related with that apparent artlessness which is one of the highest forms of art, acquire a depth of meaning far surpassing that of the spectacular shipwrecks to which the João Valérios of the literary world turn for effect. The backlander Fabiano, humble and inarticulate though he may be, takes on a stature and a dignity approaching that of figures of classic tragedy.

"Less is more," Mies van der Rohe has proclaimed. The power of Graciliano Ramos' austere creations well betokens the truth of that dictum.

RALPH EDWARD DIMMICK

CONTENTS

Barren Lives

A New Home

The jujube trees spread in two green stains across the reddish plain. The drought victims had been walking all day; they were tired and hungry. Generally they did not get very far, but after a long rest on the sands of the riverbed they had gone a good three leagues. For hours now they had been looking for some sign of shade. The foliage of the jujubes loomed in the distance, through the bare twigs of the sparse brush.

Slowly they dragged themselves in that direction. Vitória carried the younger boy astride her hip and the tin trunk on top of her head. Fabiano stumbled along gloomily, a haversack slung by its strap across his chest, a drinking gourd hanging by

3

a thong from his belt, and a flintlock resting on his shoulder. The older boy and the dog straggled along behind.

The jujubes seemed to advance, then to retreat and disappear. The older boy sat down on the ground and began to cry.

"Get going, you limb of Satan!" his father yelled at him.

As the words had no effect, he hit the boy with the scabbard of his sheath knife. The lad kicked and drew back; then, suddenly quiet, he stretched out on his back and closed his eyes. Fabiano gave him a few more whacks and waited for him to get up. He did not, however. Fabiano, looking about, cursed softly in anger.

The brushland stretched in every direction, its vaguely reddish hue broken only by white heaps of dry bones. Vultures flew in black circles over dying animals.

"Get going, you little heathen!"

The youngster did not so much as stir. Fabiano felt like killing him. His heart was heavy, and he wanted to blame his misfortune on someone. The drought seemed to him a necessary evil, and the child's obstinacy exasperated him. The boy couldn't help it if he was a hindrance, but he made going difficult and the herdsman had to get someplace or other, he didn't know where.

They had left the roads, full of thorns and stones, and for hours had been walking along the riverbed, whose dry, cracked mud scorched their feet.

The idea of abandoning the boy in that desolate spot passed through the troubled mind of the backlander. He thought of the vultures and of the piles of dry bones, and scratched his dirty red beard in indecision, examining the surroundings. Vitória stuck out her lower lip in a vague indication of direction, and uttered some guttural sounds to the effect that they were not far now. Fabiano put his knife back in its sheath and stuck it in his belt. Squatting down, he took the boy by the wrist. But the child had drawn his legs up against his belly and was as cold as a corpse. Fabiano's wrath now gave way to pity. He couldn't leave the little fellow a prey to wild animals. He handed the flintlock over to Vitória, took his son on his back, and stood up, grasping the spindling arms that dangled limply over his breast. Vitória nodded approval of this arrangement and, uttering her guttural interjection anew, pointed toward the invisible jujubes.

Thus they resumed their journey, dragging along more slowly, in great silence.

Lacking her companion, the dog took the lead. Her back

sagging, her ribs plainly visible, she trotted along panting, with her tongue hanging out. From time to time she stopped, waiting for her people, who had fallen behind.

Only the day before there had been six of them, counting the parrot. Poor thing! It had met its end on the sand of the river-bed, where they had taken their rest beside a mudhole. With no sign of food in the vicinity, hunger had been too much for the drought-sufferers. The dog had eaten the head, feet, and bones of her friend and had no more recollection of the matter. Now, standing there waiting, she looked over the family belongings and was surprised not to see on top of the tin trunk the little cage in which the bird had struggled to keep a balance.

Fabiano too missed it at times, but then he remembered: they had hunted in vain for roots to eat, the last of the manioc flour was gone, there was no sound of stray livestock to be heard in the brush.

Vitória had been seated on the warm earth, her hands crossed on her bony knees, her thoughts occupied with confused recollections of bygone days—wedding celebrations, roundups, novenas. A harsh squawk roused her from her revery and brought her back to reality. Her eye fell upon the parrot, which was spreading its claws in a fit of ridiculous fury, and without further ado she decided to make a meal of it. She justified the act by telling herself the bird was quite useless—it didn't even talk. That wasn't its fault. The family was normally one of few words, and with the coming of disaster all had fallen silent, only the briefest of utterances passing their lips. The parrot hallooed at non-existent cattle and barked like the dog.

The dark spots of the jujube trees reappeared. Fabiano's step

6

grew lighter; he forgot hunger, weariness, and sores. His rope sandals were worn at the heel; the fiber thongs had made painful cracks between his toes; the skin of his heels, though hard as a hoof, had split and was bleeding.

A bend in the road brought a fence corner into view, filling Fabiano with the hope of finding food. He felt like singing, but the only sounds he could bring forth were hoarse and rasping, and he stopped so as to save his breath.

Leaving the riverbed, they walked along the fence, climbed a slope, and arrived at the jujubes. It was a long time since they had seen any shade.

Vitória sought to make the children comfortable, covering them with rags. They had dropped to the ground like a pair of bundles. The older boy, who was now over his attack of dizziness, curled up on a heap of dry leaves, his head resting on a root. He alternately dozed and awakened. When he opened his eyes he made out vaguely a hill near by, a few stones, and an oxcart. The dog came and curled up beside him.

They were in the yard of a deserted ranch. The corral was empty, as was the goat pen. The herdsman's house was shut up. There was every indication of abandonment. Unquestionably the cattle had died and the people had moved away.

Fabiano listened in vain for the sound of a cowbell. He went up to the house, knocked, and then tried to force the door, which resisted his efforts. Crossing a garden plot in which only dead plants were to be seen, he rounded the ramshackle dwelling and came to the back yard, where he found an empty clay pit, a grove of withered catingueira trees, a turk's-head cactus, and the extension of the corral fence. He climbed up on the corner post and examined the brushland, with its heaps of bones and black clouds of vultures.

Getting down again, he tried the kitchen door without success. He turned around in discouragement and stood for a moment under the shed, considering the idea of lodging the family there. But when he came back to the jujubes he found the boys asleep and didn't want to wake them. He went to look for kindling, bringing from the goat pen a whole armload, half-eaten by termites. Pulling up some roots, he prepared to make a fire.

At this point the dog pricked up her ears and wrinkled her nose. She had caught the smell of cavies. Sniffing for a moment, she located them on the nearby hill and set off at a run.

Fabiano, gazing in the direction she had taken, gave a start: a shadow was passing over the hill! He touched his wife's arm and pointed to the sky. The two of them stood for some time staring into the light of the sun. Then, wiping away the tears that had

come to their eyes, they went and squatted by the children, sighing. There they remained crouching, dreading lest the cloud be dissipated by the fearful blue—that dazzling blue that drove people mad.

They had seen days come and go, followed by swiftly descending nights when the sky seemed to drop down, its indigo tinged only by the ruddy glow of sunset.

Infinitely small and lost in the burning desert, the two clutched at one another, making a common lot of their fears and misfortunes. Fabiano's heart beat beside that of Vitória; a weary embrace united the rags that covered them. Resisting their moment of weakness they drew apart, ashamed, but without the courage to confront the harsh light again, fearing to lose the hope they nourished.

They were aroused from the lethargy into which they were falling by the dog, who came with a cavy in her jaws. Everyone arose with a shout. The older boy rubbed the sleep from his eyes. Vitória kissed the dog's muzzle and, finding it covered with blood, licked it, profiting from her demonstration of affection.

As game the cavy was poor stuff, but it would serve to prolong life. And Fabiano wanted to live. He looked resolutely at the sky. The cloud had grown: it now covered the whole hill. Fabiano's step took on assurance; he forgot the cracks in his toes and heels.

Vitória rummaged in the trunk. The boys went to break off a branch to serve as a spit. The dog, her ears pricked up, sitting on the ground with her front paws raised, kept a watchful eye as she awaited the part that would be her lot—probably the bones, and perhaps the skin.

Fabiano took the drinking gourd and went down the slope to the riverbed. There where they had used to water the cattle he found a bit of damp earth. Digging at the sand with his fingers he waited for water to well up and then, bending to the ground, he drank at length. His thirst quenched, he lay on his back, watching the stars that were beginning to come out. One, two, three, four—there were many stars, more than he could count, in the sky. To the west it was filling up with cirrus clouds. A wild joy filled Fabiano's heart.

His thoughts turned to his family and suddenly he felt hungry. On their trek his movements had been purely mechanical, not very different, in fact, from that of the wheel of Tomás' mill. Now, as he lay there, he clutched at his belly and his teeth chattered. What had become of Tomás' mill?

He looked at the sky once more. The cirrus clouds loomed ever larger and the moon had come up, huge and white. It was surely going to rain.

Tomás too had fled from the drought and the wheel of his mill had ceased to turn. He, Fabiano, was like the mill wheel. He didn't know why, but he was.

One, two, three—there were more stars than he could count in the sky. The moon was encircled by a milky halo. It was going to rain. Good. The brush would come back to life; cattle would return to the corral, and he, Fabiano, would be the herdsman of the once-dead ranch. Bone-clappered cowbells would ring out on the lonely air. The boys, chubby and rosy-cheeked, would play in the goat pen. Vitória would have bright-flowered skirts to wear. Cows would fill the corral and the brushland would be covered with green.

He remembered that his sons, his wife, and the dog were thirsty up there under the jujube. He thought of the cavy. He filled the gourd, got up, and started off slowly so as not to spill the brackish water. As he climbed the slope a warm breeze stirred the cactus. A new beat of life sent a shiver through the brushland, through the twigs and dry leaves.

Coming up to the others he set the gourd on the ground, propping it up with stones, so that the family could satisfy its thirst. Then he squatted down, reached into the haversack, drew out the flint, and set fire to the roots he had gathered. Swelling his hollow cheeks he blew on the flames, which trembled and rose, casting a glow on his sunburned face, his ruddy beard, and his blue eyes. A few minutes later the cavy was turning and sizzling on the spit.

Happiness filled them all. Vitória would have a long flowered skirt to wear; her withered face would grow young again; her flabby haunches would fill out; her scarlet dress would be the envy of other women of the backlands.

The moon grew brighter; the milky haze surrounding it spread; the stars gradually faded in the whiteness that filled the night. One, two, three—there were only a few stars in the sky now. Close by, the cloud darkened the hillside.

The ranch would come back to life, and he, Fabiano, would be the herdsman, the real lord of that world.

Their few belongings were piled up on the ground—the flint-lock, the haversack, the drinking gourd, and the painted tin trunk. The fire crackled, and the cavy hissed on the coals.

It would be a resurrection. The colors of health would come back to Vitória's sad face. The boys would wallow in the dirt of

11

the goat pen. Cowbells would tinkle in the surroundings. The brushland would be covered with green.

The dog wagged her tail, looking at the coals. Since she couldn't be concerned with higher matters, she waited patiently for time to gnaw the bones. Afterwards she would go to sleep.

Fabiano

Fabiano was seeking to cure the wily heifer's maggot-infested sores by praying over the trail she had left. He carried a bottle of disinfectant in his haversack and if he had found the animal he would have applied treatment in the usual fashion. He couldn't find her, but he thought he made out her tracks in the sand, and squatting down he crossed two twigs on the ground and uttered an invocation. If the animal was still alive she would come back to the corral, for his prayer possessed great power.

His obligation fulfilled, Fabiano straightened up with a clear conscience and walked in the direction of the house, taking a course close to the riverbank. Soft sand was tiring to walk on, but there the hard mud made his sandals go slap-slap. The clappers of bells hanging from leather straps slung over his shoulders clinked dully. His head leaning forward, his back bent, he swung his arms to the right and left. These movements were useless, but the herdsman, his father, his grandfather, and still more remote ancestors had been used to going along narrow trails, pushing back the bushes with their hands. His sons, who were following along behind, were already beginning to imitate this hereditary gesture.

Slap-slap. The three pairs of sandals flapped against the cracked mud, dry and white on top, but soft and black underneath. The earth of the river edge gave under the weight of their feet.

The dog ran along in front, wrinkling her nose, seeking the smell of the foxy heifer in the brushland.

Fabiano was content. Yes, sir! He had fixed himself up all right. He had arrived in a terrible state, his family dying of hunger, gnawing on roots. They had dropped down in a corner of the yard under a jujube tree; later they had taken over the deserted house. He, his wife, and the boys had got used to the dark bedroom, in which they felt rather like rats, and the memory of past suffering had faded away.

He walked boldly on the cracked ground. Pulling out his sharp-pointed knife, he used it to clean his nails; then, taking from his haversack an end of rope tobacco, he crumbled it into fine bits which he rolled in a piece of cornhusk to make a cigarette. Lighting it with his tinder, he puffed away with a sense of well-being.

"Fabiano, you're a real rancher," he exclaimed aloud.

14

Then he restrained himself, noting that the boys were near by. They would surely be surprised to hear him talking to himself. Besides, thinking better of the matter, he wasn't a rancher after all; he was just another half-breed hired to look after other people's property. He was red-skinned and sunburned, had blue eyes and a ruddy beard and hair, but as he lived on other people's land and looked after other people's cattle, he considered himself a half-breed, taking off his hat and feeling ill at ease in the presence of white gentry.

He glanced around, fearful that someone besides the boys might have heard his imprudent remark. He amended it, murmuring, "Fabiano, you're a crack ranch hand." That seemed to him something to be proud of—a crack, a fellow who could handle any kind of situation.

When he had arrived at the ranch he had been in a dreadful state. And now look at him—strong, with meat on his bones, smoking his cornhusk cigarette. "Yes, sir! A crack ranch hand, Fabiano."

And he was. He had taken over the house for lack of any other lodgings and had spent a few days living on hog-plum roots and velvetbean seeds. Then the thunderstorm had come, and after that the ranch owner, who had told him to get out. But Fabiano had pretended not to understand. He had offered his services, mumbling, scratching his elbows, and exhibiting a worried smile. He was prepared to stay. And the owner had taken him on, handing over the branding irons to him.

Now Fabiano was a herdsman, and no one would drive him away. He had appeared like a stray animal, and had holed up like one. Now he was firmly planted there, more firmly than the thistles, the mandacarus, and the other cactus. He was stronger than any of them; he was like the catingueira and brauna trees. He, Vitória, the boys, and the dog were deeply rooted in the land.

Slap-slap. His sandals flapped against the cracked earth. The herdsman's body sagged, his legs were bowed, his arms dangled awkwardly at his sides. He looked like a monkey.

Sadness overtook him. What a mistake to think of himself as rooted in another man's land! His fate was to roam aimlessly up and down the world, like the Wandering Jew. He was a vagrant, driven by drought. He was only a temporary lodger there, one who had lingered on, who had taken a liking to the house, the corral, the goat pen, and the jujube that had given them shelter for a night.

He snapped his fingers. The dog came leaping to lick at his rough, hairy hands. Fabiano was touched by the animal's show of affection.

"You're a fine dog, you are."

Living far from other men, he got along well only with animals. His feet were hard enough to crush thorns and be quite insensitive to heat. His walk, however, was awkward; he leaned first to one side and then to the other in an ugly, lopsided twist, whereas on horseback he was one with the steed, as if glued to it. His was a sing-song language of guttural monosyllables, of cries and interjections, which his animal companions had no trouble in understanding and with which he occasionally addressed humans. In all truth, he spoke very little. He marveled at the long, difficult words used by town folk, and sought vainly to repeat some of them, though he knew they were useless and perhaps dangerous.

One of the children came up to him with a question. Fabiano stopped, wrinkled his brow, and waited for the question to be repeated. Not understanding what the boy wanted, he took him to task. The boy was becoming entirely too curious. If he kept up that way, nosing into things that were none of his business, what would become of him? He shooed the boy away in annoyance.

"These little devils seem to have the idea that—"

He did not complete the thought. He had decided that he was wrong. He tried to recall his own childhood. He saw himself as a stunted youngster in a dirty, torn shirt, tagging along after his father as he did the field chores, asking him questions that got no answers. He called to the boys, talked to them of things near by, and sought to arouse their interest. He clapped his hands and gave a cry.

"Sic 'em!"

The dog dashed off through the runners and thistles, trying to smell out the foxy heifer. After a few minutes she came back, sad and dejected, her tail drooping. Fabiano consoled her with a pat. He had only wanted to teach the boys something. It was good for them to know that this was the way they should act.

He took longer strides and, leaving the dry mud of the river edge, came to the slope that led to the yard. He was disturbed. A cloud darkened his blue eyes. It was as if an abyss had opened in his life. He needed to talk to his wife, to shake off his perturbation, to fill up the baskets, to give pieces of saguaro to the cattle. Fortunately the heifer had been cured by his prayer. If she died, it would not be his fault.

The boys cried out as their father had done, "Sic 'em!" and the dog dashed off once more into the bushes, again in vain. The children were amused and excited, and Fabiano's spirits brightened. That was right. The dog couldn't find the heifer in the bushes, but it was good for the boys to get used to the easy exercise, clapping their hands, shouting, and following the movements of the animal. The dog came back, her tongue hanging out, panting. Fabiano took the lead, satisfied with his lesson, and thinking of the mare he was to break—one that had never been shod or had worn a saddle. There was going to be an awful commotion in the brush!

Right now he wanted to have a talk with Vitória about the boys' upbringing. Certainly she was not to blame. Busy with the housework, watering the pinks and the pots of wormwood, taking the empty jar down to the stream and bringing it back once she had filled it, she left the boys free to play in the clay pit, as muddy as pigs. And they were at the unbearable age when they asked one question after another. Fabiano was perfectly content to be ignorant. Did he have a right to know anything? No.

If he learned anything at all, he would need to know more and would never be satisfied. That was the rub.

He recalled Tomás the miller. Of all the men of the backlands, Tomás the miller had been the most completely ruined. Why? It could only be because he read too much. Fabiano had often said to him, "Tomás, you're touched in the head. Why all this paper? When trouble comes, you'll be in just as bad a fix as everyone else." Well, the drought had come, and the poor old man, with all his goodness and all his book learning, had lost everything and had had to take to the road, with nowhere to go. Perhaps he had already given up the ghost. A person of his kind couldn't stand a long, hard summer.

To be sure, his knowledge inspired respect. When Tomás the miller went by, yellow, hunchbacked, and pensive on his slow, blind horse, Fabiano and his likes took off their hats. Tomás answered by touching the brim of his straw hat, turning from one side to the other, his legs bowing in their black boots with red patches.

In moments of madness, Fabiano tried to imitate him. He mouthed big words, which he got all wrong, and tried to convince himself he was improving. This was nonsense. It was perfectly obvious that a fellow like him was never intended to talk properly.

Tomás the miller talked properly. He wore his eyes out over books and newspapers, but he didn't know how to order people to do things. He asked them instead. There was something queer about so much politeness from a man who was well-to-do. People even criticized such ways. But they all obeyed Tomás. Who said they didn't?

Other gentry were different. His present boss, for instance, yelled over nothing at all. He almost never came to the ranch, and when he did it was only to find fault with everything. The cattle were increasing and the work was going well, but the boss bawled the herdsman out. It was quite natural: he bawled him out because his position permitted him to, and Fabiano listened with his hat under his arm, making excuses and promising to do better. All the while he was swearing to himself he would do just as before, because everything was in order and the boss only wanted to show his authority and yell that the place was his. Who said it wasn't?

Fabiano was just part of the ranch equipment, a tool of little value; he would be dismissed when he least expected it. When he was hired he was furnished with a horse and with leg and chest protectors, a jacket, and heavy shoes, all of untanned leather, but when he left he would hand all these over to the herdsman who took his place.

Vitória wanted a bed like Tomás the miller's. This was sheer madness. He didn't say anything, so as not to hurt her feelings, but he knew it was madness. Luxuries weren't for ranch hands. Besides, they were there only temporarily. Any day the boss might turn them out, and they would have to take to the road, with no place to go and no way of carting around household possessions. Their bundles were always made, and they could sleep quite well under a tree.

He looked out over the yellow brush, which the setting sun tinged with red. If drought came, not one green plant would be left. A shiver ran over him. Of course it would come. It had always been that way, as long as he could remember. And even before he could remember, before he had been born, there had been good years mixed with bad years. Misfortune was on the way; perhaps it was near at hand. It really wasn't worth while working. There he was, walking toward the house, climbing the slope, kicking pebbles out of the way with his sandals, and disaster was coming at a gallop, aiming to get him.

Turning so as not to arouse the boys' curiosity, he crossed himself. He didn't want to die. He still planned to travel, to see a little of the world, and to meet important people like Tomás the miller. His was a bad lot, but Fabiano was determined to struggle against it and felt strong enough to come out the winner. He didn't want to die. He was hidden in the brush like an armadillo—as hard and as clumsy as an armadillo. Some day, though, he would come out of his hiding place and walk with his head up, his own boss.

"Your own boss, Fabiano."

He scratched the stubble of beard on his chin, stopped, and relit his cigarette. No, he would probably never be his own boss. He would always be just what he was now, a half-breed, ordered around by gentry, little more than a piece of livestock on another man's ranch.

But afterwards? Fabiano was sure it wouldn't be over so soon. He had gone days without eating, tightening his belt, drawing in his stomach. He would live for years, for a century. But if he should die of hunger or on the horns of a bull, he would leave sturdy sons who would beget sons of their own.

Everything around was dry and harsh. And the boss was harsh too, peevish, exacting, thieving, and as ticklish to handle as a spiny cactus.

It was of prime importance for his sons to get started on the right road, learning to cut saguaro for the cattle, to repair fences, and to break horses. They had to be hard, like armadillos. If they didn't become calloused they would come to the same end as Tomás the miller. Poor fellow! What use had all his books and newspapers been to him? He had died of a sick stomach and weak legs.

Some day— Yes, when droughts went away and everything

21

ran right— But would droughts ever go away and things run right? He didn't know. Tomás the miller must have read about that. Free of that danger the boys could talk, ask questions, and do anything they liked. But now they had to behave like the kind of people they were.

He came to the yard, where he could make out the low, dark house with its black tile roof. Behind him were the jujube trees, the pile of stones on which they threw dead snakes, and the oxcart. The boys' sandals flapped on the smooth, whitish ground. The dog trotted along panting, with her mouth open.

At that hour of the day Vitória must be in the kitchen, squatting beside the stones on which she did the cooking, her flowered skirt gathered up around her thighs, fixing dinner. Fabiano was hungry. After the meal he would talk with her about the boys' upbringing.

22

Jail

Fabiano had gone to the market in town to buy supplies. He needed salt, manioc flour, beans, and brown sugar. Vitória had also asked for a bottle of kerosene and a cut of red calico, but the kerosene Inácio sold was mixed with water and the calico of the sample cost too much.

Fabiano went from store to store, picking over the cloth, trying to beat the price down a fraction, fearful of being cheated. Long years of mistrustfulness were revealed in his hesitant gestures. At one point in the afternoon, half-tempted, he pulled out his money. Then he quickly changed his mind, sure that all the clerks were cheating both on the price and on the measure. He tied up the bills in the corner of his handkerchief, stuck it in his pocket, and headed for Inácio's tavern, where he had stored his duffel.

There he proved once more to his satisfaction that the kerosene had been watered. Feeling hot, he decided to have a drink. Inácio brought the bottle of rum. Fabiano downed his glass at one swallow, spat, wiped his lips on his sleeve, and frowned. He could swear that the rum was watered. Why did Inácio have to water everything, he wondered. Gathering up his courage, he questioned the tavern keeper.

"Why do you water everything?"

Inácio pretended not to hear.

Fabiano went and squatted on the sidewalk, feeling in a mood for conversation. His vocabulary was limited but in moments of expansion he had recourse to some of the expressions used by Tomás the miller. Poor Tomás! Such a fine man to go drifting off like a mere hired hand, with a bundle on his back! Tomás was a man to be respected; he was a registered voter. Who would have thought this could happen?

At this moment a policeman dressed in khaki came up and gave Fabiano a friendly swat on the shoulder.

"How about it, fellow?" he asked. "Want to go in and have a game of cards?"

Fabiano eyed the uniform with respect and, trying to recall some of the expressions of Tomás the miller, he stammered, "Yes and no. That is— I mean— Provided— Well, if you like."

He got up and followed the man in khaki, the representative of the law, the giver of orders. Fabiano had always obeyed. He was strong and muscular, but he was little given to thought. He asked for little, and obeyed.

The two walked through the tavern and down a hall to a room where several men were playing cards on a mat.

"Move over," said the policeman. "You have company."

The card players drew closer together; the two newcomers sat down, and the policeman in khaki picked up the deck. It was not his lucky day. He was soon in the hole and so was Fabiano. Vitória would be furious, and with good reason.

"Serves me right!"

He rose to his feet angrily and left the room scowling.

"Hey, wait there, fellow!" the man in khaki called.

Fabiano, his ears burning, did not even turn his head. He asked Inácio for his belongings, slipped into his leather jacket, put his arms through the straps of his haversack, and went out into the street.

He stopped under the courbaril tree in the square to talk to Rita, the pottery seller. He didn't dare go home. What excuse could he give to Vitória? He got hopelessly involved in inventions: he had lost the package of cloth; he had paid for a bottle of something at the pharmacy for Rita the pottery seller. It was no use; he was all mixed up. He had a poor imagination and he was no good at lying. In all the stories he made up in his defense the figure of Rita appeared, and this annoyed him. He was determined he would think up something in which she had no part. He would say that the money for the calico had been stolen. After all, wasn't it true? The other players had swindled him at cards. But he mustn't mention the game. He would say merely that the handkerchief with the bills had disappeared from the pocket of his leather jacket. He would say: "I bought the provisions. I left the jacket and the saddlebags at Inácio's tavern. I met up with a policeman in khaki." No, he hadn't met anyone. He was all mixed up again. He wanted to make the policeman out to be an old acquaintance, a childhood friend. His wife would get all puffed up over this. But then again, maybe she wouldn't. She was smart and would see he was just bragging. Well then, the money had slipped out of his jacket pocket at Inácio's tavern. That was perfectly natural.

He was repeating to himself that it was perfectly natural when someone shoved him against the courbaril tree. The market was breaking up. It was growing dark and the lamplighter, climbing up on his ladder, was turning on the streetlights. The evening star shone over the church tower. The judge went to take his stand at the door of the pharmacy, where he would hold forth to an admiring circle. The tax collector limped by, with the stubs of his receipts under his arm. The garbage wagon rolled across the square, gathering up fruit rinds. The priest came out of his house, raising his umbrella for protection against the damp night air. Rita went her way.

Fabiano shivered. It would be night by the time he got back to the ranch. Wrapped up in that cursed game, befuddled with the rum he had drunk, he had let time slip by. And since he wasn't taking any kerosene, for the next week they would have to depend on pieces of torchwood for light at night. He straightened himself up, ready to get on his way.

Another shove sent him off balance. He turned around and saw beside him the policeman in khaki, staring at him defiantly, his face a rusty red, his brow wrinkled in a frown. Fabiano started to shake his leather hat in the face of his attacker. With one well-aimed blow with that hat he could knock the little runt to the ground. But he looked at the people and things around him and his indignation died down. Out on the range he was cock of the walk, but on the streets in town he sang another tune.

"Is that any way to treat a peaceful citizen?" he asked.

"Get going!" bellowed the policeman, and he insulted Fabiano for leaving the tavern without saying goodbye.

"Don't be a f-fool," stammered the backlander. "Is it my fault if you lost your shirt playing cards?"

He choked. The representative of the law circled around for a minute, trying to pick a quarrel. Finding no pretext, he came up and planted the heel of his boot on the herdsman's canvas sandal.

"That's no way to act," Fabiano protested. "I'm not bothering anybody. People's feet are tender."

The policeman ground his heel down harder and harder. Losing his temper, Fabiano made an insulting reference to the man's mother. At once the khaki-clad adversary blew his whistle, and in a matter of minutes the town police force had the courbaril tree surrounded. "On your way!" the corporal shouted.

Fabiano moved without knowing where he was going, found himself in jail, listened without understanding to a charge made against him, and offered no defense.

"All right," said the corporal. "Down you go, fellow!"

Fabiano fell on his knees and was whacked on his back and chest with the flat side of a broad knife. Then a door was opened and he was given a shove that landed him in the darkness of a cell. The key rasped in the lock. Fabiano got up in a daze, stumbled, and went to sit down in a corner, muttering to himself.

Why had they done that to him? He couldn't figure it out. He was a well-behaved citizen, yes sir! He had never been arrested. And here, before he knew it, he was mixed up in a brawl for no reason at all. He was so upset he couldn't believe it was true. They had all jumped on him without any warning, the bastards! They didn't give a man a chance to defend himself.

"Oh well—" There was nothing he could do. He ran his hands over his chest and shoulders. He felt completely done in. His bluish eyes shone like those of a cat. Yes, he really had been beaten and thrown in jail. But it was such a queer business that a few minutes later he was again shaking his head in disbelief, despite his bruises.

The policeman in khaki— Yes, there was a guy in khaki, a

good-for-nothing that he, Fabiano, could have knocked all apart with one good slap. He hadn't, though, because he represented the law. Fabiano spat scornfully.

"The dirty, low-down runt!"

For the sake of a skunk like that they beat up the father of a family! He thought of his wife, the boys, the dog. Crawling on hands and knees, he hunted for the saddlebags, which had fallen on the floor. He made certain that all the things he had bought at the market were still there. Something might have got lost in the confusion. He remembered a piece of goods he had seen at the last shop he visited—pretty, stoutly woven, wide, with flowers on a red background. Just what Vitória wanted. And by being stingy, by trying to beat down the price a bit, he had come to this at the end of the day!

He fished around in the saddlebags again. Vitória would be worried about his not coming home. The house would be dark, the boys would be sitting by the fire, the dog would be keeping watch. They had certainly barred the front door.

He stretched out his legs and leaned his sore back against the wall. If they had given him time, he would have explained everything perfectly. Taken by surprise, though, he hadn't known what to say. Who would have, under the circumstances? He couldn't convince himself that the brutality had been directed at him. It was a mistake; the policeman in khaki had confused him with someone else. That was the only explanation.

Just because some worthless troublemaker got peeved, did they have to go and throw a fellow in jail and beat him up? He knew perfectly well that was the way things were. He was used to violence and injustice. And he had consoled such of his acquaintances as spent the night in the stocks or endured whipping saying, "Don't worry. It's no disgrace to take a beating from the law."

But now he ground his teeth. He sighed. Did he deserve to be punished?

Try as he might, he could not be convinced that the policeman in khaki was really the law. The law was something far off and perfect; it couldn't make mistakes. The policeman in khaki was right there, on the other side of the bars; he was wicked and weak; he played cards with country people and then picked quarrels with them. Surely the law could not permit such evil.

After all, what good were policemen in their khaki uniforms? He kicked the wall and cried out in fury. What good were policemen? The other prisoners stirred; the jailer came up to the bars of the cell, and Fabiano calmed down. "All right, all right. Nothing's the matter."

But a lot of things were the matter. He just couldn't explain them. They could ask Tomás the miller, who read books and knew what was what. Tomás the miller could explain that business, but he, Fabiano, dull fool that he was, could not. He just wanted to go home to Vitória and lie down on their bed of tree branches. Why did they have to make trouble for somebody who only wanted to rest? Why didn't they go bother someone else? It was all wrong.

Did they have real courage? He tried to imagine the policeman in his khaki uniform attacking a bandit out in the brushland. What a laugh! A policeman that fell into a bandit's hands wouldn't even leave a grease spot.

He thought of the old house where he lived, of the kitchen, of the kettle singing on the stones that held it off the fire. Vitória would be putting salt in her cooking. He opened the saddlebags again. The package of salt had not got lost. Good! Vitória would be tasting the soup, sipping from her coconut-shell ladle. And Fabiano was vexed because of her, because of the boys, because of the dog, who was like a member of the family, as smart as a person. On that long trek, at the time of the great drought, when they were all starving, the dog had brought them a cavy. It was getting old now, poor thing. Vitória would be worried and would be going often to listen at the front door. The rooster would flap his wings, the goats would bleat in their pen; the bells of the cows would tinkle.

If only— But what was he thinking of? He looked out the grating into the street. Lord but it was dark! The light on the corner had gone out, probably because the man with the ladder had put in only half a quart of kerosene.

Poor Vitória, worrying there in the dark, the boys sitting by the fire, the kettle hissing on the stones, the dog on watch, the tin lamp hanging from a peg that stuck out of the wall—

He was so tired, and ached so, that he was on the point of going to sleep despite all his misfortune. A drunk was ranting in a loud voice, and some men were squatting around a fire that filled the jail with smoke,. arguing and complaining about the damp wood.

Fabiano nodded. His head dropped heavily to his chest, then snapped back. He ought to have bought the kerosene from Inácio. His wife and boys would get smoke in their eyes from the torchwood.

He awoke with a start. Wasn't he mixing things up, losing his mind? Perhaps it was the effect of the rum. No, it wasn't. He had drunk just one glass—four fingers. If they would give him time he could explain how it all happened.

As he listened to the disjointed raving of the drunk, a painful doubt assailed him. He too said things that had no sense or meaning. Angry at the comparison, he beat his head against the wall. He was stupid, yes; he had never had any schooling; he didn't know how to explain himself. Was he in jail for that? How was it then? Do you put a man in jail because he doesn't know how to explain things right? What was wrong with his being stupid? He worked like a slave, day in and day out. He cleaned out the watering trough, he mended the fences, he treated the stock for ailments. He had put life into an empty shell of a ranch. Everything was in order. They could see for themselves. Was it his fault he was stupid? Who was to blame?

If it hadn't been— He didn't know. The thread of the idea grew—grew, and then broke. It was hard to think. He spent so much time with animals. He had never seen a school. That was why he couldn't defend himself, why he couldn't put things in their proper place. He no sooner got that devilish business in his head than it slipped out again. It was enough to drive a man crazy. If they had only given him some schooling, he could understand it. But it was no use. He only knew how to deal with animals.

And yet— Tomás could tell them. They should go ask him. He was a good man, Tomás the miller. He had book learning. Well, every man was as God had made him. He, Fabiano, was just plain dumb.

What he wanted— He forgot what he wanted. His thoughts

now were turning to the journey he had made across the backland, ready to drop from hunger. The boys' legs were as thin as
rails; Vitória stumbled repeatedly under the weight of the trunk
with their belongings. On the riverbank, from necessity, they
had eaten the parrot that didn't know how to talk.

Fabiano didn't know how to talk either. Sometimes he came
out with a big word, but it was all a fake. He knew perfectly well
it was foolish. He didn't know how to set his thoughts in order.
If he did, he would go out and fight policemen in khaki uniforms
who beat up harmless people.

He beat on his head and pressed it in his hands. What were
those guys doing squatting around the fire? What was that drunk
saying who was bellowing at the top of his lungs, wasting his
breath? Fabiano wanted to cry out, to yell that they were no
good. He heard a thin voice. Someone in the women's cell was
crying and cursing the fleas. Some whore probably, the kind that
would take on anybody. She was no good either. Fabiano wanted
to yell to the whole town, to the judge, the chief of police, the
priest, and the tax collector, that nobody in there was worth a
damn. He, the men squatting around the fire, the drunk, the
woman with the fleas—they were all completely worthless, fit
only to be hanged. That was what he wanted to say.

But there was that running fire that came and went in his
spirit. Yes, there was that. But just what was it? He needed to
rest. His head ached, probably from being hit with a knife handle. His head hurt all over; it seemed as if it were on fire, as if a
kettle were boiling in his brain.

Poor Vitória, worried, but trying to calm the children. The dog
on the alert, beside the fire. If it weren't for them—

At last Fabiano was managing to put his thoughts in order. What held him was his family. He was tied down, like a calf lashed to a stake for branding. If it weren't for that, no policeman in khaki would tramp on his foot! What softened him was the thought of his wife and boys. Without their yoke upon him he would not bend his back. He would leave that place like a tiger and go out and do something wild. He would load his musket and put a shot into that policeman in khaki. No, the policeman was a poor devil who didn't deserve so much as a smack from the back of his hand. He would kill the people from whom the policeman took his orders. He would join a gang of bandits and wipe those people out. He wouldn't leave one of them to raise a family. That was the thought that was boiling in his head. But there was his wife, there were the boys, there was the dog.

Fabiano gave a yell, scaring the drunk, the men who were fanning the fire, the jailer, and the woman who was complaining about the fleas. He had that yoke on his neck. Should he continue to bear it? Vitória would be sleeping uneasily on her bed of tree branches. The boys were stupid like their father. When they grew up they would herd cattle for a boss they never saw; they would be stepped on, abused, and hurt by a policeman in a khaki uniform.

Vitória

Squatting beside the stones that served her as a trivet, her flowered skirt tucked up between her legs, Vitória was blowing on the fire. A cloud of ashes rose from the embers, covering her face. Smoke filled her eyes; her rosary of blue and white beads slipped from her bosom and banged against the kettle. Vitória wiped the tears from her eyes with the back of her hand, wrinkled her eyelids, poked her rosary back in her dress, and, puffing out her cheeks, continued to blow with a will.

Flames licked at the firewood, died down, then sprang up once more, and spread between the stones. Vitória straightened her back and began using a fan. A shower of sparks arose, casting a glow on the dog, who was curled up asleep, lulled by the heat and the smell of the cooking.

Feeling the draft and hearing the crackling of the tinder, the dog awoke and drew back prudently, fearful lest a spark land on her coat. She looked in wonder at the little red stars that died out before touching the ground. She wagged her tail in approval of the spectacle and then sought to express her admiration to her mistress by jumping up, panting, and standing on her hind legs as if she were a person. Vitória, however, was in no mood for appreciation.

"Get!" she cried, and kicked at the dog, who withdrew in humiliation and with feelings of revolt.

Vitória had got out on the wrong side of the bed that morning. Without the slightest provocation she had made some rude remarks to her husband about the bed of tree branches on which they slept. Fabiano, who had not been expecting such an outburst, merely grunted. Since woman is a very difficult animal to understand, he took flight, going to stretch out in the hammock, where he again fell asleep. Vitória had walked back and forth, looking for something on which she could vent her spleen, but as she found everything in order she had been reduced to complaining about life in general. Now she took revenge on the dog by giving her a kick.

She looked out the low kitchen window at the boys, happy in the dirt, covered with mud, making clay oxen which they set to dry in the sun under the Jerusalem thorn. She could find no reason for taking them to task. She thought again of the tree-branch bed and mentally cursed Fabiano. Yes, they slept on that thing; they had got used to it; but it would be better to sleep on a leather-bottomed bed, like other people.

She had been talking to her husband about this for more than a year now. Fabiano first agreed with her, and went mulling over figures that came out all wrong. So much for the leather, so much for the frame. Well, they could get the bed, he said finally, by saving on clothes and kerosene. Vitória declared that was impossible. The two of them were badly enough dressed as it was, and the children ran around naked. They all went to bed early. You might say they never lit a lamp in the house. They had discussed the matter, seeing whether they could cut expenses somewhere else, but, as they couldn't reach any agreement, Vitória had made a caustic reference to the money her husband spent at the market on cards and rum. Piqued, Fabiano had reproached her for the patent-leather shoes she wore on feast days. They were expensive and useless. Stumbling along in them she swayed like a parrot, looking utterly ridiculous. Vitória was greatly offended by the comparison, and had it not been for the awe in which Fabiano held her, she would have told him a thing or two. As a matter of fact the shoes did hurt her feet and give her calluses. Trying to walk on the high heels she could hardly keep her balance. She stumbled and limped, and probably did look ridiculous, but to hear Fabiano say so hurt her deeply.

The cloud having passed, her bitterness swallowed, the bed again loomed up on her limited horizon. Right now she was thinking of it ill-humoredly. She felt it was something she would never have. She mixed it up in her mind with her household chores.

Vitória slipped into the sitting room, ducked under the end of the hammock in which Fabiano lay snoring, took from the corner shelf her pipe and a cake of tobacco, and went out into the yard. The bell of the red cow tinkled down by the river. She

wondered whether Fabiano had remembered its treatment. She thought of waking him up and asking him, but her attention was attracted to the prickly pears and the mandacarus that stood out on the range.

A shimmering haze rose from the scorched earth. She trembled, recalling the drought; her dark face grew pale; her black eyes widened. She strove to drive away the remembrance, fearful lest it become a reality. She muttered a Hail Mary under her breath, then, feeling more tranquil, she found her attention drawn to a hole in the fence around the goat pen. She crumbled the cake of tobacco between the palms of her hardened hands, filled her clay pipe, and went to mend the fence. Coming back, she circled the house, crossed the little enclosure at the side, and went into the kitchen.

"Fabiano may have forgotten about the red cow."

She squatted down, stirred up the fire, picked up a coal with a spoon, lit her pipe, and began to pull on the bamboo stem, clogged with tobacco tar. She took a long spit out through the window and into the yard, and prepared to take another. For some strange reason, the act linked itself in her mind with the thought of the bed. If her spit reached the yard, the bed would be bought before the end of the year. She filled her mouth with saliva, leaned forward—and missed. She tried several times, but to no avail. The only result was that she ran out of spit. She arose in disappointment. It was nonsense; there was no point to it.

She went to the corner where the water jar stood on a three-legged support and drank a mugful. The water was brackish.

"Ugh!"

Two images came to her mind simultaneously: pots and water

holes. Mingling in confusion, they canceled each other out. Vitória laid her index finger on her brow in perplexity. What was she trying to think of? She looked at the ground in concentration, trying to remember, and saw her feet, big and flat, with widely separated toes. Suddenly the two ideas came back to her: the water hole was drying up and the contents of the pot hadn't been seasoned.

She raised the lid and a burst of steam rose in her red face. Wasn't she letting the food burn? She added water and stirred with the black coconut-shell dipper. Then she tried the broth. It was tasteless—no food for a Christian. She went to the hanging shelf where they kept slabs of sun-dried meat and other provisions, opened the bag of salt, took a handful, and tossed it in the kettle.

Then her thoughts turned to the water hole, with its dark liquid which the animals refused to drink. The only thing she feared was a drought.

She looked again at her spreading toes. Really, she couldn't get used to wearing shoes, but just the same Fabiano's gibe had hurt. Feet like a parrot! Well, probably so. That's the way it is with country people. But why did he have to hurt her feelings? The comparison rankled.

The poor parrot. It had journeyed with her in the cage that swayed on top of the tin trunk. It would stutter, "Pretty birdie." That was all it knew how to say. The only other sounds it made were imitations of Fabiano's calls to the cattle and the dog's bark. Poor thing. Vitória didn't even want to think about it. She had forgotten her former life; it was as if she had been born after her arrival at the ranch. The reference to her shoes had opened an old wound, and the trip had come back to her mind. Her sandals had been worn out on the stones. Weary, half-dead of hunger, she carried the younger boy, the trunk, and the parrot cage.

Fabiano was mean. "Ungrateful wretch!"

She looked at her feet again. The poor parrot. She had killed it on the riverbank, out of necessity, to feed her family. At the moment the parrot was angry, keeping a firm eye on the dog, hopping along unsteadily, like country folks on a feast day. Why did Fabiano have to bring that memory back to her?

She went to the door and looked at the yellow leaves of the brush. She sighed. Surely God would not permit another such misfortune. She shook her head and sought other matters to occupy her mind. She took the big gourd, went to the mudhole, filled the chickens' dish with water, and straightened their perch. Then she went to the garden to water the pinks and the pots of wormwood. And she chased the boys into the house. They were covered with mud from head to toe.

"You little devils!" she scolded. "You're as dirty as pigs. You look as if you had been—"

She stopped. She was going to say they looked as if they had been playing in the bottom of a parrot's cage.

Escaping, the boys went and rolled themselves up in the straw mat from the sitting-room floor, under the corner shelf. Vitória went back to the fire and relighted her pipe. The pot was hissing. A sultry, dusty breeze shook the cobwebs that hung like curtains from the roof beams. The dog, under the hanging shelf, bit at fleas and snapped at flies. Fabiano's even snoring was plainly to be heard and its rhythm was not without influence on

41

Vitória's thoughts. Fabiano was snoring with assurance: chances were there was no danger; drought was far off.

Once again Vitória set to thinking of the leather-bottomed bed. The dream, however, was linked in her mind to the recollection of the parrot, and she had to make a great effort to separate out the object of her desire.

Everything there was stable and sure. Fabiano's snoring, the crackling of the fire, the tinkling of the cowbells, even the buzzing of the flies gave her a feeling of firmness and repose.

Would she have to sleep all her life on a bed of tree branches? Right in the middle of the bed there was a knot, a big bump in the wood. She curled up on one side and her husband on the other. They couldn't stretch out in the middle. At first she hadn't minded. Limp, exhausted from work, she could have lain on a bed of nails. Now, however, they had begun to be a bit more prosperous. They were eating and putting on weight. To be sure, they didn't own anything. If they left, they would take with them their clothes, the shotgun, the tin trunk, and a few odds and ends. But they were getting along, by the grace of God. The boss trusted them. They could almost consider themselves fortunate. All they lacked was a bed. That was what tormented Vitória. Since she was no longer worn out with hard work, she spent part of the night thinking. That business of turning in as soon as it was dark wasn't right though. People aren't the same as chickens.

At this point Vitória's thoughts took another road, which, however, shortly led back to the first one. The fox had made off with the black and white hen—the black and white one, the plumpest of all! She decided to set a trap near the perch. Her dander was up. That fox would pay for the black and white hen. "The thief!"

Gradually her annoyance took still another direction. Fabiano's snoring was unbearable. Nobody snored the way he did! It would be a good idea to get up and look for another tree branch to take the place of that one that didn't let a body turn over. Why hadn't they replaced that pesky branch? She sighed. They couldn't make up their minds. Well, she would just have to be patient. It was better to forget about the knot and think of a bed like the one that belonged to Tomás the miller. Tomás had a real bed, made by a carpenter, with a frame of sucupira wood, smoothed with an adze, the dovetails cut out with a chisel and neatly fitted together, the frame covered with a rawhide, well stretched and nailed down. That was a bed on which a Christian could stretch his bones!

Suppose they sold the chickens and the young sow? Unfortunately the fox had got the black and white hen, the one with the most meat on it. She was going to have to teach that fox a lesson. She was going to set a trap by the perch and break the wretch's back.

She got up, went to the bedroom to look for something, and came back discouraged having forgotten what it was she went for. Where was her head?

She sat down by the low kitchen window, discontent. She would sell the chickens and the sow and she would stop buying kerosene. It was no use consulting Fabiano, who was always enthusiastically making plans which he then quickly abandoned.

She wrinkled her brow, startled with her idea, but sure that her husband would be pleased with owning a bed. Vitória wanted a real bed, of leather and sucupira wood, just like Tomás the miller's.

The Younger Boy

He got the idea the afternoon Fabiano put harness on the sorrel mare and started to break it. It wasn't really an idea; it was just a vague hankering to do something new and different, something which would impress his brother and the dog.

At the moment he was filled with admiration for Fabiano. Dressed all in leather—chaps, jacket, and chest protector—he seemed like the most important man in the world. The rowels of his spurs jingled in the yard. His hat, held by a strap under his chin, was pushed back on his head, its broad brim making an enormous frame around his sunburned face.

The horse was saddled, the stirrups securely attached, and Vitória was holding it by the head to keep it quiet. The herdsman tightened the cinch and circled slowly around the animal, checking all the fastenings. Without so much as a jerk he avoided a kick, turning his body so that the mare's hoofs passed by his chest, grazing the jacket. Then he climbed up on the shed and leaped into the saddle. His wife drew back, and there was a whirlwind in the brush.

The younger boy clambered up on the corral gate and, wringing his sweaty hands, stretched to get a better view of the cloud of dust that blanketed the imburana trees. He stayed that way for what seemed an eternity, filled with mingled joy and fear, until at last the mare came back to the yard and began to buck furiously, as if the very devil were in her. Suddenly the cinch broke and everything came apart. The boy gave a cry and all but fell off the gate. He recovered his calm at once, however, for Fabiano had landed on his feet and was walking away unsteadily on his bandy legs, with the harness over his arm. The stirrups, which had come loose in the wild ride, bumped against each other, and the rowels of Fabiano's spurs clinked.

Vitória was calmly smoking her pipe, seated on the bench under the shed, as she looked for lice in the older boy's hair. The younger boy couldn't endure such indifference to his father's prowess. He went to wake up the dog, who was stretched out lazily, her red belly shamelessly exposed. The dog opened one eye, leaned her head against the grindstone, yawned, and went back to sleep.

Finding the dog stupid and self-centered the boy left her in indignation and went to pull at his mother's sleeve, seeking to

46

get her attention. Vitória uttered an exclamation of annoyance and then, when the youngster insisted, gave him a crack on the skull.

The boy strode away angrily and leaned against one of the posts that supported the shed roof. The world was full of evil; it made no sense. He went to the goat pen, where the animals bleated and sniffed, raising their wrinkled noses. They seemed so funny to the boy that he forgot the dog's egotism and Vitória's ill humor. His admiration for Fabiano, however, continued to grow.

Misunderstandings and rude words vanished from his mind as real enthusiasm filled his small breast. Though he was afraid of his father, he came slowly up to him, rubbed against his chaps, and touched the tail of his jacket. The chaps, the jacket, the chest protector, the spurs, and the hat with its chin strap seemed marvelous to him.

Fabiano brushed the boy aside without noticing him and went into the sitting room to divest himself of his grandeur.

The boy lay down on the straw mat, curled up, and closed his eyes. Fabiano filled him with awe. On the ground, stripped of his leather garments, he was less impressive, but astride the sorrel mare he was a frightening spectacle.

The boy went to sleep and dreamed. A gust of wind covered the leaves of the imburana trees with dust, Vitória went on with her hunt for lice on the head of the older boy, the dog continued asleep with her head on the grindstone.

The next day all these images were swept away completely. The jujubes at the end of the ranch yard were dark, standing out from the other trees. Why? the boy wondered.

Approaching the goat pen he saw the old billy goat, his nostrils dilated, making an ugly noise, and the happenings of the day before came back to him. He walked over to the jujubes, bending forward, trying to make out the tracks of the sorrel mare.

At lunch time Vitória scolded him. "That little imp is out of his head," she declared.

The boy got up, left the kitchen, and went to look at the chaps, the chest protector, and the jacket, hanging on a wooden peg in the sitting room. Then he walked over to the goat pen, and there the plan was born.

At first he turned back. He had a mind to go talk to someone, but he didn't know what he wanted to say. The images of the sorrel mare and the billy goat mingled in confusion in his mind, as did those of himself and his father.

He circled the goat pen like a vulture, imitating Fabiano.

He felt a need to consult his brother, but then he thought better of the matter. The older boy would laugh and make fun of him—and go tell Vitória. He was afraid of being laughed at and made fun of. And if his brother told on him Vitória would pull his ears.

Obviously he wasn't Fabiano. But supposing he were? He needed to show that he could be Fabiano. If only he had someone to talk to, perhaps he could explain himself.

He walked around a bit aimlessly until his brother and the dog took the goats to the water hole. The gate opened, a stench spread over the surroundings, the bells tinkled. The boy in his little cotton shirt moved across the ranch yard, rounded the rock pile where they threw dead snakes, passed the jujubes, went down the slope, and arrived at the riverbank.

The goats were pushing and shoving, sticking their noses in

the water, their horns clattering against each other. The dog ran around barking busily.

Climbing up on the bank, his heart beating wildly, the younger boy waited for the billy goat to come down to the water hole. It was a risky business, but it seemed to him that up there he was taller and could be another Fabiano.

He couldn't make up his mind though. The billy goat would surely buck and throw him.

He straightened up and started away, almost free of the temptation. He saw a flock of parakeets flying over the brush. He would have liked to get hold of one, tie a string to its leg, and feed it. The parakeets disappeared, screeching, and the boy was left sadly scanning the cloud-filled sky. Some of the clouds looked at first like little sheep, but then they lost that shape and took on those of other animals. Two big ones came together; one looked like the sorrel mare; the other like Fabiano.

The boy lowered his sun-blinded eyes, rubbed them, and again approached the riverbank, from which he could view the confused mass of the flock and hear the clatter of horn on horn. If the billy goat had already drunk he was going to be disappointed. He examined his spindling legs and his dirty, torn shirt. He had made out figures of living beings in the sky and was convinced that mysterious forces would come to his aid. He would float in the air, like a parakeet.

He began to bleat, imitating the goats, calling to his brother and the dog. Meeting with no response, he felt resentful. He was going to show the two of them something that would send them back to the house full of amazement.

At this point the billy goat approached and stuck its nose in the water. The boy leaped from the bank and landed astride its back.

He dug into the soft hair, slipped, tried in vain to get a hold with his heels. He was thrown forward and then back, and found himself straddling the animal's hindquarters. The goat was bucking wildly, probably backing away from the water hole. The boy leaned to one side, but a violent shake brought him back to an upright position. Then a mad dance began, in which his arms and legs waved helplessly in the air. Thrown forward once again, he gave a somersault over the goat's head, tearing his shirt still further on one of the horns, and landed sprawling in the sand. There he lay, flat and motionless, his ears buzzing. He was vaguely conscious that he had escaped from his adventure without honor.

Gazing at the clouds which were dissolving in the sky, he took a sudden dislike to them. The flight of the vultures, however, caught his attention. Fabiano, when he walked along swaying under the weight of his leather outfit, looked just like a vulture.

The boy sat up and felt his sore joints. He had been violently shaken and felt as if his bones had been pulled all apart.

He looked angrily at his brother and the dog. They should have warned him. They didn't show the slightest sign of sympathy. His brother was laughing like a fool. The dog, with a serious air, seemed to disapprove of the whole business. He felt puny and abandoned, the victim of falls, kicks, and butts.

He got up and dragged himself dispiritedly to the fence around the water hole, against which he leaned, his face toward the muddy water, his heart despondent. Running his fingers through the rip in his shirt he scratched his thin chest. The flock

of goats disappeared up the slope; the dog barked in the distance. What would the clouds be like? Probably some were taking on the shape of lambs, others those of unknown animals.

The thought of Fabiano came to his mind and he sought to banish it. Fabiano and Vitória were certainly going to punish him for the accident. He raised his eyes timidly. The moon had appeared and loomed up large, accompanied by an all-but-invisible star. By this time the parakeets must be resting in the dry clumps of corn in the river flat. If he only had one of those parakeets, he would be happy.

He lowered his head and looked again at the dark water hole that the livestock had emptied. A few thin streams of water oozed out of the sand, like blood from the veins of animals. He remembered the goats he had seen slaughtered with a mallet and hung bleeding, head down, from a beam of the shed.

He withdrew. His feeling of humiliation gradually disappeared and died. He had to go into the house, eat, and sleep. And he had to grow up, to become as tall as Fabiano, to kill goats with a mallet, to wear a pointed knife in his belt. He was going to grow, stretch out on a bed of tree branches, smoke corn-husk cigarettes, and wear shoes of untanned leather.

He climbed the slope and slowly approached the house, giving a twist to his legs and swaying as he walked. When he was grown to be a man he would walk like that, heavily, swaying, with an air of importance, the rowels of his spurs jingling. He would leap on the back of an untamed horse and go flying across the brushland like a gust of wind, raising a cloud of dust. Coming back he would jump to the ground and walk across the ranch yard like this, bowlegged, with his leather chaps, jacket, chest protector, and hat with a chin strap. The older boy and the dog would be filled with admiration.

The Older Boy

It all happened because Vitória wouldn't take a minute to talk to the older boy. Nobody had ever mentioned Hell in his hearing before, and, surprised at old Miss Terta's language, he asked for an explanation. Vitória, whose attention was on other matters, said vaguely that Hell was a very bad place, and when the boy asked her to describe it she merely shrugged her shoulders.

The boy went into the sitting room to ask his father. He found him sitting on the floor with his legs spread apart, unrolling a piece of shoe leather.

"Put your foot there," he ordered.

The boy did as directed and Fabiano took the measure for a sandal, making a knife mark behind the heel and another in front of the big toe. After outlining the sole of the foot, he gave a clap of his hands and said,

"Take your foot away."

The boy stepped back, but remained circling around, and at last timidly risked his question. Getting no reply, he went back to the kitchen and tugged at his mother's skirt.

"What's it like?" he asked.

Vitória said it was full of red-hot spits and bonfires.

"Did you see them?"

Irritated by what she considered insolence, Vitória gave him a crack on the skull.

Indignant at the injustice, the boy left the house, crossed the yard, and took refuge under the dry catingueira trees beside the empty pond.

The dog was his companion in that hour of trial. She had been stretched out beside the stones on which Vitória did the cooking, drowsing in the heat, waiting for a bone. In all probability she wouldn't get one, but she believed in bones and she found the state of torpor enjoyable. She stirred a bit from time to time, raising to her mistress black eyes shining with confidence. Having accepted the idea that there might be a bone in the kettle, she was not going to let anybody or anything disturb her modest hopes. She got an occasional kick for no reason at all. The kicks were to be expected and did nothing to dispel the vision of the bone.

Vitória's strident voice and the crack on the older boy's skull roused the dog from her torpor, however, and made her suspect that things were not going well. She went and hid in a corner behind the mortar, making herself small among the baskets.

56

After a minute or so she raised her muzzle, trying to decide where to go. The warm wind blowing from the direction of the pond tipped the balance for her. She slipped along the wall, jumped out the low kitchen window, crossed the yard, passed under the Jerusalem thorn, and came upon her companion weeping unhappily in the shade of the catingueiras. She tried to comfort him by leaping and bounding about him and wagging her tail. She wasn't particularly happy, but on the other hand she couldn't abide excessive grief. Since she was not one to lose patience easily, she kept up her leaping and panting, trying to attract her friend's attention. Finally she convinced him that his weeping was useless.

He sat up, cuddled the dog's head in his lap, and started in a low voice to tell her a story. His vocabulary was almost as limited as that of the parrot that had died during the drought. As a result, he had recourse to exclamations and gestures, and the dog replied by wagging her tail and licking at him with her tongue, and making other movements that were easily understood.

Everyone else had abandoned him; the dog was the only living being that felt any sympathy for him. He stroked her with his thin, grubby fingers and the animal curled up the better to enjoy the pleasant contact, which gave her a feeling not unlike that which she received from the warm ashes of the fire.

The boy went on petting her and lowering his dirty face to her muzzle he stared deep into her calm eyes.

He had been playing in the clay pit with his brother, making toy oxen, and was smeared all over with mud. Abandoning his pastime, he had gone to question Vitória. What a mistake! The fault was all old Miss Terta's. The evening before, after saying a prayer to cure the pain in Fabiano's chest, she had come out with a strange word. She hissed when she talked, with her pipestem firmly clamped between her toothless gums. The boy wanted a clear idea of what the word meant, and he was disappointed when his mother talked about a bad place with spits and bonfires. Hence he had protested, hoping she would change Hell into something else.

All the places he knew were good: the goat pen, the corral, the clay pit, the yard, the water hole. This was a world peopled by real beings—the herdsman's family and the ranch animals. Beyond this world there were the blue hills that rose in the distance, the ridge where the dog went to hunt cavies, the brushland with its all but imperceptible trails, its isolated clumps of trees, and its impenetrable thickets of macambira. This was another world, populated by stones and plants, each with a life of its own, just like people. These two worlds lived in peace with one another. At times the frontier between them was broken down. The inhabitants on either side understood each other and lent each other a helping hand. There were undoubtedly evil forces at work everywhere, but they were always overcome. When Fabiano was breaking an untamed horse there was obviously a guardian spirit that kept him in the saddle, that showed him the least dangerous trails, that delivered him from thorns and sharp branches.

The relations between the two worlds had not always been friendly. A long time back his people had had to flee, without knowing where, weary and hungry. Vitória, with the younger boy astride her hip, balanced the tin trunk on her head, Fabiano carried the flintlock on his shoulder, the dog trotted along with her ribs plainly visible through the thin hair of her flanks. He, the older boy, had fallen on the ground, which was burning his feet. Everything had gone dark all of a sudden, the cactus had disappeared, he had scarcely felt the whacks Fabiano gave him with his knife sheath.

In those days the world was a bad place. But then it had grown better. You might say the bad things had never existed. On the hanging shelf in the kitchen slabs of sun-dried beef were lined up beside pieces of pork fat. His people were no longer tormented by thirst, and in the afternoon when the gate was opened the goats and other small stock ran down to the water hole. Bones and stones were occasionally transformed into beings that peopled the tree clumps, the ridge, the distant hills, and the macambira thickets.

As he didn't know how to talk properly, the boy babbled complicated expressions, repeated syllables, imitated the cries of the animals, the noise of the wind, the sound of the branches creaking together out in the brush. Just now the boy had thought he was going to learn a word that must be important, since it figured in old Miss Terta's conversation. He was going to memorize it and pass it on to his brother and the dog. The dog wouldn't be impressed, but his brother would admire and envy him.

"Hell, Hell—"

He couldn't believe that a word with so musical a ring could be the name of something bad. He had decided to argue with Vitória. If she had said that she had been there, all well and good. Vitória's authority was visible and powerful, and made itself felt. It would have been all right too if she had referred to some higher, invisible power. But she had tried to convince him

by giving him a crack on the head, and this struck him as absurd. Knocks were natural when grownups were angry; he even thought their ill-humor was the sole cause of all the raps and ear-pullings he received. This belief made him distrustful and caused him to observe his parents carefully before speaking to them. He had gathered up courage to address Vitória because she was in a good mood. He explained this to the dog with an abundance of cries and gestures.

The dog detested violent displays of emotion. She stretched her legs, closed her eyes, and yawned. As far as she was concerned, kicks were a disagreeable and necessary fact of existence. There was only one means of avoiding them: flight. At times, however, she was taken by surprise and the toe of a sandal found its way to her rump. Then she would go yelping to hide in the woods, filled with a desire to bite at ankles. Since she could not attain her wish, she would calm down. The fuss her friend was making was unreasonable. She again stretched out her legs and gaped. It would be nice to have a nap.

The boy kissed her damp muzzle and rocked her. His thoughts turned to the blue hills and the macambira thickets. Fabiano said there were cougars' dens in the hills and that the flat heads of vipers rose up amid the macambira thorns.

He rubbed his thin hands and scratched at his dirty nails. He thought of the little figures of oxen he had left by the clay pit, but this brought the unfortunate word back to his mind. He tried to get his fatal curiosity out of his head, pretending he hadn't asked the question and hence had not received the rap.

He got up. He saw the kitchen window and through it the bun of Vitória's hair. This brought evil thoughts to his mind. He went and sat down behind another tree from which he could see the line of hills, covered with clouds. At dusk the hills melted into the sky and the stars moved across them. How could there be stars on the earth?

The dog came bounding up to him, sniffing at him and licking his hands, then settled down beside him.

How could there be stars on the earth?

He felt sad. Perhaps Vitória had told the truth. Hell must be full of vipers and cougars, and the people who lived there must always be getting raps on the head, tugs at their ears, and whacks with knife sheaths.

Despite having changed his position, he couldn't get the thought of Vitória out of his mind. He told himself again that nothing had happened and tried to think of the stars whose lights appeared on the line of hills. It was no use. At that hour the stars were not yet out.

He felt weak and helpless. He looked at his thin arms and bony fingers and began to make mysterious drawings on the ground. Why had Vitória said that?

He hugged the dog so hard it hurt. She didn't like to be hugged. She preferred to leap and to roll on the ground. Smelling the kettle, she dilated her nostrils and reproved her friend for his strange ways. A big bone was bobbing up and down in the soup. This consoling thought would not leave her.

The boy continued to embrace her. The dog, so as not to hurt his feelings, curled up and submitted to his excess of affection. He smelled good, but his smell was mixed with that of the kitchen. There was a big bone there, full of marrow, and with a little meat on it.

Winter

The family was gathered around the fire. Fabiano sat on the overturned mortar; Vitória was on the ground, with her legs crossed and the boys' heads on her knees. The dog had lifted her head to look at the coals, which were gradually graying with ash.

It was bitterly cold. Outside the gutters dripped, the wind shook the branches of the catingueira trees, and the roar of the river was like distant thunder.

Fabiano rubbed his hands in satisfaction and pushed at the burning wood with the toes of his sandal. The coals flared up, the ash fell away, and a circle of light spread about the stones that served as a trivet, casting a vague glow on the herdsman's feet, his wife's knees, and the stretched-out children. From time to time the latter stirred, for the fire was a small one and warmed only parts of their bodies. Other parts felt the chill air that came in through the chinks in the walls and cracks in the window. This kept them from going to sleep. Just as they were about to drowse off, a shiver would make them turn over. They would pull nearer the fire and give ear to what their parents were saying. It wasn't really a conversation, just a series of isolated phrases, marked by repetitions and incongruities. Sometimes a guttural interjection lent force to a sentence of ambiguous meaning. The fact was that neither of the parents was paying any attention to the words of the other. They were merely giving vent to the thoughts that passed through their minds, thoughts which followed one another in confusion, thoughts which they could not master. As their means of dealing with them were limited, they sought to make up for the deficiency by talking aloud.

Fabiano rubbed his hands again and began a rather unintelligible story, but as only his sandals were in the circle of light, the gesture went unnoticed. The older boy pricked up his ears attentively. If he could see his father's face, perhaps he would understand part of the story; it was hard for him to do so in the dark. He got up and fetched an armload of wood from a corner of the kitchen. Vitória gave a grunt of approval at the action, but Fabiano, who didn't like to be interrupted, saw in it a lack of respect and stretched out his arm to cuff the boy. The lad slipped out of reach and rolled his mother's skirt about him. Vitória frankly took his side.

"Humph! What a temper!"

That was the way her man was—constantly ready to fly off the handle.

"Always exploding over something."

She stirred the ashes with the handle of her coconut-shell ladle and pushed damp pieces of mimosa wood in between the stones, trying to get them to catch. Fabiano came to her aid. Ceasing his talk, he got down on all fours and blew on the coals, puffing out his cheeks mightily. Smoke filled the kitchen and they all coughed and rubbed their eyes. Vitória fanned, and in a few minutes flames were sputtering between the stones.

The circle of light grew. Now the faces loomed redly out of the shadows. Fabiano, visible from the belt down, faded into an indistinct black mass above, lit only by occasional flickers. From this dark mass came once more the mumble of his words.

Fabiano was in a good mood. Some days earlier the rising waters of the river had covered the posts set at the end of the river flats and reached the catingueira trees, which now must be submerged. Surely only the topmost leaves could be showing and the rising foam would be eating away the banks.

It wouldn't be long before that deluge was gone, but Fabiano wasn't thinking of the future. Right now the flood was rising, drowning animals, filling the hollows, and overflowing the meadowlands. Good! Fabiano rubbed his hands. No longer was there the fear of an immediate drought which had terrified the family for months. The brush had turned yellow and then rusty brown, the cattle had begun to grow thin, and horrible nightmares had filled the family's dreams. Then suddenly a thin line of lightning had broken the sky toward the headwaters of the river. Other, brighter flashes had followed; thunder had rumbled near at hand; in the midnight darkness blood-colored clouds scudded across the sky. Gale winds tore up sucupira and imburana trees, and lightning came so thick and fast that Vitória and the children sought refuge under the covers in the bedroom, stopping up their ears. The wild gale suddenly ceased, however; rain began to fall; and the head of the flood appeared, dragging with it tree trunks and the bodies of animals. The water rose, it covered the path that led up the bank, it seemed as if it would reach the jujubes at the back of the yard. Vitória was frightened. Was it possible that it would get up to the jujubes? If that happened, the house would be flooded too, and the family would have to climb the hill and camp out a few days there, living like cavies.

She sighed and stirred the fire with the handle of the coconut-shell ladle. Surely God would not permit such a misfortune. The house was strong. She sighed again. The posts were of pepperwood, firmly set in the hard ground. If the river reached the house it would only wash away the mud that filled in the cracks in the wattles. God would protect the family. Again she sighed.

The wattle walls were firmly anchored; the frame of the house would resist the fury of the waters. And when they went down, the family would return. Yes, they would all live in the woods like cavies, but they would come back when the waters went down, and they would take mud from the clay pit to cover the skeleton of the house. She sighed.

Vitória fanned briskly so as not to hear the noise of the approaching river. Was it really going to rise still more? The fan swished, and the sound of the flood was like a breath that died away on the other side of the jujubes.

Fabiano was telling of great deeds he had done. He began

modestly, but he gradually warmed to the subject, and taking an exaggeratedly optimistic view of the events he came to the conviction that he had performed some real feats. He needed such a conviction. Not long before there had been that trouble with the policeman at the market, who had provoked him, beaten him with the flat of his knife, and thrown him in jail. Fabiano had gone around blue for weeks, imagining various kinds of revenge, seeing the stock waste away on the baking brushland. If a drought came, he would leave his wife and sons and would cut the policeman to bits. Afterwards he would kill the judge, the district attorney, and the chief of police. He had been that way for days, dejected, thinking of the drought, and with the recollection of his humiliation gnawing at his soul.

But then the rumble of thunder had come, followed by the floodwaters, and now the gutters were dripping and the wind was coming in through the holes in the walls.

Fabiano rubbed his hands in contentment. As the cold was great, he drew nearer to the flames. He was telling of a terrible brawl. He had forgotten about jail and the beating he had taken, and felt he was capable of great deeds.

The river was coming up the slope; it was near the jujubes. There was no report that it had ever reached them, however, and Fabiano, secure in the information he had had from old-timers, was telling the tale of a fight he had won. The fight was purely imaginary but Fabiano believed in it.

The cows had come for shelter to the side of the house by the corral. The rain lashed them; their bells clanged. They would get fat on the new grass and would have calves. Grass would grow in the fields, the trees would take on new leaves, the cattle would multiply. They would all put on weight—Fabiano, his wife, their two sons, and the dog. Perhaps Vitória would have her leather-bottomed bed. Really, the bunk of tree branches on which they slept was anything but comfortable.

Fabiano made gestures, while Vitória continued fanning the flames that rose from the damp mimosa. The boys, hot on one side and cold on the other, unable to sleep, lent an ear to their father's tall tale. They began in a low voice to discuss an obscure point of the story. Unable to come to agreement, they grew angry and were on the point of blows. Fabiano, annoyed at their impertinence, thought of punishing them, but then, calming down, he repeated, with different words, the part they hadn't understood.

The younger boy clapped his hands as he watched by the light of the flickering flames Fabiano's agitated gestures. The backs of Fabiano's hands remained in the shadow, but the palms shone bloodred in the light. They looked as if he had just finished flaying an animal. His tangled, ruddy beard could not be seen; his bluish eyes stared fixedly at the burning brands; his harsh, hoarse voice lapsed from time to time into silence. Fabiano sat on the mortar, his body sagging, ugly and coarse, like that of an animal too heavy to stand on two feet.

The older boy was not satisfied. Since he couldn't make out his father's features he closed his eyes, the better to understand what he was saying. But a doubt had crept into his mind. Fabiano had changed the story, and that lessened its verisimilitude. The boy was disenchanted. He stretched and yawned. It would have been better for Fabiano to have repeated the same words. He would have argued with his brother over their meaning. They would have fought over the words and the conviction of his rightness would have grown. Fabiano should have repeated the words. But no, instead he had introduced a variation, and the hero had become a common man, with common human contradictions.

The older boy remembered a toy he had once possessed, a present from Tomás the miller. He closed his eyes and then opened them, but they were heavy with sleep. The draft that came in through the cracks in the wall chilled one of his arms and legs—his whole right side. He turned over, and the parts of Fabiano which had been visible vanished from his sight. The toy had got broken, and the youngster had wept over the useless pieces. He remembered the little corrals he had built of small pebbles, under the catingueira trees. Now the pond was full and had spread over the corrals he had made. The clay pit too was full; its water reached to the kitchen wall and mingled with that of the pond. In order to get to the garden plot, with its pinks and pots of wormwood, Vitória had to go out the front door, down past the shed, through the brauna-wood gate. Behind the house, the fences, the Jerusalem thorn, and the catingueiras were standing in water. The gutters dripped, the cowbells clanged, the toads croaked. The sound of the cowbells was familiar, but the voices of the toads and the drip of the gutters were strange to' his ears. Everything was different. It rained all day and all night. The thickets and clumps of trees in which mysterious creatures dwelled had been violated. There were toads out there. Their music rose and fell and a mournful cadence filled the surrounding air. The boy tried to count the voices, but got mixed up. There were too many of them, more toads than anyone could count out in the thickets and among the trees. What could they be doing? What was the meaning of their sad, croaking tune? He had never seen a toad, and he confused them with the invisible inhabitants of the hills and the clumps of macambira. He curled up, made himself comfortable, and went to sleep, one side warmed by the fire, the other protected by Vitória's thighs.

The fan waved back and forth; the damp wood hissed; Fabiano's face first shone in the light and then disappeared in the darkness.

The dog, motionless and patient, stared into the coals and waited for the family to go to bed. The noise Fabiano was making wearied her. Out in the fields, following a steer, he could yell his lungs out. That was natural. But here beside the fire, why should he be shouting so? Fabiano was wasting his breath for no purpose at all. The dog was sick of it. She tried to doze off, but couldn't sleep. Vitória should take out the coals and the ashes, sweep the floor, and go to bed with Fabiano. The boys would settle themselves on the straw mat under the corner shelf in the sitting room. It would be nice if they would leave her in peace. She spent the whole day watching people's movements, trying to understand incomprehensible things. Now she needed to sleep, to get rid of her fleas, to be freed from the vigilance to which they had accustomed her. Once the ground had been swept with the broom she would slip in among the stones, curl up and go to sleep in their heat, with the smell of the damp goats in her nostrils and strange noises in her ears—the drip-drip of the water from the eaves, the toads' chorus, and the roar of the swollen river. Small, ownerless insects would come to pay her a visit.

Feast Day

Fabiano, Vitória, and the boys were going to the Christmas celebrations in town. It was three in the afternoon and exceedingly hot; small whirlwinds spread clouds of dust and dry leaves over the yellowed trees.

They had closed up the house, crossed the yard, gone down the slope, and were stumbling along on the stones, like sore-hoofed oxen. Fabiano, cramped in the suit of duck old Miss Terta had sewed for him, wearing a baize hat, a collar and tie, and thin-leather gaiters, tried to hold himself straight, something he did not ordinarily do. Vitória, clad in her red, flowered dress, had a hard time keeping her balance in her high-heeled shoes. She insisted on wearing the kind city girls did, and she stumbled as she went along. The boys were wearing jackets and trousers for the first time. At home they wore just a little shirt of stripped cotton or else went naked. Fabiano, however, had bought ten ells of white cloth at the store and had charged old Miss Terta with making suits for him and his boys. Old Miss Terta had said the cloth was hardly enough, but Fabiano had paid no attention, sure she only intended to steal the scraps. As a result the suits were short and tight, and showed much patching.

Fabiano tried to overlook these disadvantages. He walked along stiffly, his belly sticking out and his shoulders thrown back, gazing at the distant range of hills. Normally he looked at the ground, so as to avoid stones, stumps, holes, and snakes. The forced posture wearied him. When he got to the sand of the riverbed he realized he could never go the three leagues to town that way. He pulled off his gaiters, stuffed his socks in his pocket,

took off his coat, collar, and necktie, and heaved a sigh of relief. Vitória decided to follow his example. She took off her shoes and stockings, tying them up in her kerchief. The children put their sandals under their arms and felt quite at ease.

The dog, who had been tagging along behind, joined the group at this point. If she had appeared sooner, in all probability Fabiano would have chased her back and she would have spent the holiday with the goats that dirtied the shed with their droppings. With his collar and tie rumpled in his pocket, his coat over his shoulder, and his gaiters on the end of a stick, the herdsman felt closer to her and accepted her company.

He resumed his normal stance, walking with a sway, his head bent forward. Vitória, the two boys, and the dog accompanied him. The afternoon went by rapidly, and by nightfall they were at the creek bank where the street began.

There Fabiano stopped, sat down, and washed his horny feet, striving to get the dirt out of their deep cracks. Without drying, he tried to put his gaiters and socks on. It was a struggle: the heels of the cotton socks got balled up on his instep and the thin-leather gaiters resisted like shy virgins. Vitória pulled up her skirt, sat down on the ground, and likewise washed. The two boys waded into the brook, where they scrubbed their feet, then got out, put on their sandals, and stood watching their parents' movements. Vitória finished and got up, but Fabiano was puffing with exasperation. He had overcome the obstinacy of one of those cursed gaiters, but the other was stuck and all his tugs on the straps were in vain.

Vitória offered suggestions which only served to irritate her husband. There was no way of getting his heel down where it belonged. A harder pull on the strap at the back caused it to break off in his hand. Fabiano energetically grasped at the elastic instead, but to no avail. He got up, resolved to start down the street like that, limping, with one leg longer than the other. In rage, mingled with hope, he gave a violent stamp on the ground. His flesh squeezed, his bones cracked, his damp sock tore, and his cramped foot slipped into place in its leather prison. Fabiano heaved a long sigh of relief and pain. Then he tried to fasten his hard collar around his neck, but his trembling fingers weren't equal to the task. Vitória came to his aid; the collar button slipped into its little hole and the tie was knotted. Their dirty, sweaty hands left black marks on the collar.

"It's all right now," grunted Fabiano.

They crossed the plank bridge and started down the street. Vitória stumbled as she walked, because of her high heels, and held her umbrella, handle down, ferrule up, wrapped in her kerchief. It would be impossible to say why she carried it handle down. She herself could not have explained it. She had always seen other country women do thus and she had adopted the custom.

Fabiano marched along stiffly.

The two boys stared at the street lamps and divined wonders. They were afraid, rather than curious, and consequently walked softly, lest they attract other people's attention. They had always supposed there were worlds different from that of the ranch, marvelous worlds in the blue hills. This, however, was peculiar. How could there be so many houses and so many people? Surely the men were going to have a fight. Would these people be hostile and forbid them to go in among the stands? They were used to having their ears pulled and their heads cracked. Perhaps the strangers wouldn't whack them as Vitória did, but the youngsters shrank back, clung to the walls, half-dazzled, their ears full of strange sounds.

They arrived at the church and went in. The dog stayed trotting around on the sidewalk, looking at the street with distrust. In her opinion everything ought to be dark, because it was night, and the people walking in the square should go to bed. Raising her muzzle, she noted an odor that made her want to cough. They were making entirely too much noise around there and the light was too bright, but what really bothered her was that smell of smoke.

The boys too were astonished. In their suddenly expanded world Fabiano and Vitória loomed up much less impressively: they were smaller than the figures on the altars. The boys didn't know what altars were, but they gathered that the objects on them must be precious. The lights and the singing enchanted them. The only light on the ranch was that of the kitchen fire and the kerosene lamp that hung by its handle from a peg in the wall; the only singing consisted of Vitória's blessing and Fabiano's halloos. The halloo was sad-sounding, a monotonous, wordless tune that lulled the cattle.

Fabiano remained staring at the images and the lighted candles in silence. He was uncomfortable in his new suit; he held his neck stretched and walked as if on coals. The crowd cramped and hampered him more than his suit. When he had his chaps, jacket, and chest protector on, he was boxed in like an armadillo in its shell, but he could leap on the back of an animal and go flying off across the brushland. Now he couldn't even turn around; hands and arms brushed against his body. He remembered the beating he had taken and the night he had spent in jail. The feeling he now had wasn't very different from that which he had experienced as a prisoner. It was as if the hands and arms of the crowd were trying to grab hold of him, subdue him, and press him into a corner. He looked at the faces around him. Obviously the people who had gathered there didn't notice him, but Fabiano felt as if he were surrounded by enemies; he feared he might get into arguments and that the night might end badly. He puffed and tried uselessly to fan himself with his hat. It was difficult to move; he was practically tied. Slowly he managed to make his way through the throng, slipping over to the holy-water font, where he stopped, fearful of losing sight of his wife and sons. He stood on tiptoe but this only brought a groan from him: his blistered heels were beginning to hurt. He made out the bun of Vitória's hair. She was more or less hidden by a pillar. Probably the boys were with her. The church got fuller and fuller. To make out his wife's head, Fabiano had to stretch and turn his own. And his collar was digging into his neck. The gaiters and the collar were indispensable. He couldn't go to the novena wearing sandals and a cotton shirt, open in front, exposing his hairy chest. That would be a lack of respect. Since he had religion he went to church once a year, and as long as he could remember he had seen people dress like this on feast days, in starched trousers and jacket, gaiters, baize hat, collar, and necktie. He would not risk breaking tradition, even if he suffered for it. He thought he was performing a duty. He tried to straighten up, but his will flagged. His spine sagged naturally, and his arms dangled awkwardly.

76

Comparing himself with the city folk, Fabiano held himself inferior. This was why he was afraid the others would make fun of him. He assumed a surly expression and avoided conversations. People talked to him only to get something out of him. The tradesmen cheated on measure, price, and accounts. The boss's figuring with pen and ink he could not understand; the last time he met with him there had been some confusion about numbers, and Fabiano, his brain awhirl, had left the office in indignation, sure he had been cheated. He took a beating from all of them. The clerks, the tradesmen, and the landowner stole the shirt off his back, and those who had no dealings with him laughed when they saw him go stumbling down the street. This was why Fabiano tried to avoid those people. He knew his new suit, cut and sewed by old Miss Terta, his collar, his tie, his gaiters, and his baize hat made him look ridiculous, but he didn't want to think about that.

"Lazy, thieving, gossiping, good-for-nothings!"

He was convinced that all the town folk were evil. He bit his lips. He couldn't afford to say anything like that. For a much lesser offence he had been whacked with a knife and had had to sleep in jail. Now that policeman in khaki— He shook his head to get rid of the unpleasant recollection and sought for a friendly face in the crowd. If he found someone he knew, he would call him out on the sidewalk, embrace him, smile, and clap his hands. Then they would talk about cattle. He shivered, and tried to make out the bun of Vitória's hair. He had to be careful not to get too far from his wife and children. He moved in their direction and came up to them at the moment that the church was beginning to empty.

Pushing and shoving they made their way out and down the steps. Bumped and jostled, Fabiano again thought of the policeman in khaki. Out in the square, on passing by the courbaril tree he turned his face away. For no reason at all the wretch had gone and provoked him, stepping on his foot. He had turned away, politely. But since the other fellow had persisted, he had lost his patience and had flown off the handle. The result: he had been whacked on the back with a knife and had spent a night in jail.

He invited his wife and the boys to take a ride on the merry-go-round, saw them seated, and amused himself for a while watching them ride by. Then he went to the gambling booths. He scratched, pulled out his handkerchief, untied it and counted his money, tempted to risk it on a game of dice. If he were lucky he could buy the bed of untanned leather his wife dreamed of. He went and had a drink of rum at one of the stands, came back, and circled around in indecision, looking at Vitória in a mute appeal for her opinion. She made a gesture of disapproval and Fabiano withdrew, remembering the game at Inácio's with the policeman in khaki. He had been cheated; he was sure he had been cheated. He went back to the stand and had another drink of rum. Little by little he lost his inhibitions.

"Feast days a fellow has to celebrate," he declared.

He had still one more drink; then, straightening up, he stared at the passers-by in defiance. He was resolved to do something crazy. If he came on the policeman in khaki there would be a real row. He walked around among the stands, swaggering, kicking at the ground, oblivious of the blisters on his feet. He was looking for trouble: he wanted to show that good-for-nothing! He paid no attention to his wife and sons, who were following him.

"I'd like to see a real man!" he bawled.

In the hubbub of the square no one heard the challenge, and Fabiano withdrew behind the stands, to the other side of the vendors of sweetmeats. He was in a mean mood but not entirely without a sense of prudence. There back of the stands he could give vent to wrath and spout threats and insults at invisible enemies. Driven by opposing forces, he took certain precautions in exposing himself. He knew that an outburst was dangerous; he was afraid the policeman in khaki might appear suddenly and tramp on his foot with his boot. The policeman was a paltry fellow, but he acted brave in the company of his companions. It was a good idea to avoid him. The thought of him at times was unbearable though, and Fabiano was getting even. Stimulated by the rum he had drunk, he grew bold.

"Where is that bully? I'd like to see a fellow with nerve enough to say I'm ugly! Aren't there any real men around here?"

He stammered out his challenge with a vague fear of being heard. No one appeared. Fabiano blustered and shouted they were all lily-livered cowards. Yes they were! After a lot of yelling, supposing there were men there, hiding from fear of him, he insulted them,

"Pack of—"

He stopped in an agony of cold sweat, his mouth full of saliva, unable to find the right word. A pack of what? He had the word on the tip of his tongue, but that tongue was swollen and stiff. Fabiano spat and fixed glassy eyes on his wife and boys. He drew back a few steps, with a feeling of nausea. Then he again approached the area of bright lights, limping, and went and sat down on the sidewalk in front of a store. He felt limp and dispirited; his enthusiasm had chilled. A pack of what? He repeated his question, without knowing what he was seeking. He looked closely at his wife's face but couldn't make out her features. Could Vitória be aware of his fluster? There were other back-country men there talking, and Fabiano found them disgusting. If he didn't feel so qualmish, belching and sweating, he would get into a fight with them. His mind, already befuddled by the question that was troubling him, was further bothered by the thought that those people had no right to sit on the sidewalk. He wanted them to leave him alone with his wife, his boys, and the dog. A pack of what? He gave a harsh cry and slapped his hands together.

"A pack of dogs!"

Having discovered the expression that had so stubbornly eluded him, he was elated. A pack of dogs. Obviously, back-country people like him were no better than dogs. He reached with his hands for his wife and boys and found they were seated beside him. A violent cramp in his neck made his face twist in pain and his mouth again filled with saliva. He started to spit. Calmer, he breathed deeply and wiped a thread of saliva from his chin with his fingers. He was dizzy, and had an annoying buzzing in his ears. He was going to swear that he had been in danger and had shown courage, but at the same time he felt he had done wrong.

Now he was sluggish and drowsy. While he had been showing off, with a head full of rum, he had paid no attention to the blisters on his feet. Now that he had calmed down, the gaiters hurt entirely too much. He pulled them off, took off his socks, got rid of his collar, tie, and coat, which he rolled up into a pillow, and, stretching out on the sidewalk, he pulled his baize hat over his eyes and went to sleep with a queasy stomach.

Vitória was in difficulties; there was a certain necessary matter she needed urgently to attend to and she didn't know how to go about it. She might seek concealment at the other side of the square, behind the stands and the stools on which the vendors of sweetmeats sat. She arose, her mind half made up, then squatted down again. Could she leave the boys with her husband in that state? She restrained herself, looking desperately in every direction, for her need was great. She slipped away unobtrusively and came to the corner of the store, where a crowd of women were squatting. And, staring at the house fronts and the paper lanterns, she wet the ground and the feet of the other country women. She made her way slowly back to her family, took from her pocket her clay pipe, packed and lit it, and gave long puffs of satisfaction. Having relieved herself, she looked with interest at the people swarming in the square, the auction table, and the bright trails of the rockets. Really, life wasn't too bad. She gave a shiver as she thought of the drought, of the terrible trek they had made under the burning sun, seeing nothing but bones and twisted branches. She wiped the recollection from her mind, turning to the beautiful things there at hand. The noise of the crowd was pleasant to hear; the drone of the hurdy-gurdy at the merry-go-round never ceased. All Vitória needed for life to be good was a bed like Tomás the miller's. She sighed, thinking of the bed of tree branches on which they slept, and squatted there smoking, her eyes and ears wide open so as to lose nothing of the festivities.

The boys exchanged impressions in a whisper, worried at the disappearance of the dog. They tugged at their mother's sleeve. What could have happened to the dog? Vitória raised her arm in a vague gesture and pointed in a couple of directions with the stem of her pipe. The boys persisted in their questioning. Where could the dog be? Indifferent to the church, the paper lanterns, the stands with things for sale, the gaming tables, and the rockets, they concentrated solely on the legs of the passers-by. Poor thing, she must be lost among them, getting kicked by all those feet.

Suddenly the dog appeared. She jumped up on the sidewalk, dived through the women's skirts, climbed over Fabiano, and came up to her friends, her tongue and tail manifesting a lively contentment. The older boy grabbed her. She was safe! They tried to make her understand that they had been greatly worried about her, but she paid no attention to their explanation. She just thought they were wasting time in a funny place full of strange odors. She felt like barking in opposition to all this, but realizing that she wouldn't win anyone to her way of thinking she dropped her tail and curled up, resigned to the caprices of her masters.

The boys were of an opinion similar to hers. Looking at the stores, the stands, and the auction table, they conferred together in amazement. They had accepted the fact that there were a lot of people in the world, and now they busied themselves with

the discovery of a huge number of things. They discussed in a whisper the surprises with which they were filled. It was impossible to imagine so many marvelous things all at one time. The younger boy timidly expressed a doubt to his brother: Could all that have been made by people? The older boy hesitated. He looked at the stores, at the stands with their lights, and at the girls in their pretty dresses. He shrugged his shoulders. Perhaps it had all been made by people. Then a new problem presented itself to his mind and he whispered it in his brother's ear: In all probability those things had names. The younger boy looked at him questioningly. Yes, surely all the precious things exhibited on the altars and on the shelves in the stores had names.

They began to discuss the perplexing question. How could men keep so many words in their heads? It was impossible; no one could have so vast a store of knowledge. Free of names, things seemed distant and mysterious. They had not been made by people and it was imprudent for people to meddle with them. Seen from afar they were pretty. Filled with admiration and awe the boys talked in low voices so as not to unleash the strange forces the things might contain.

The dog was drowsing. From time to time she shook her head and wrinkled her muzzle. The city was full of smells of sweat which she found disconcertingly unfamiliar.

Vitória seemed to see amid the stands the bed of Tomás the miller—a real, honest-to-goodness bed.

Fabiano, lying on his back, snored, the brim of his hat covering his eyes, his head resting on his thin-leather gaiters. He was having a nightmare, and the dog noted that he gave off a smell which rendered him unrecognizable. Fabiano tossed and made noises. Many policemen in khaki had appeared and were trampling on his feet with enormous military boots, threatening him with terrible knives.

The Dog

The dog was dying. She had grown thin and her hair had fallen out in several spots. Her ribs showed through the pink skin and flies covered dark blotches that suppurated and bled. Sores on her mouth and swollen lips made it hard for her to eat and drink.

Fabiano, thinking she was coming down with rabies, tied a rosary of burnt corncob about her neck. The dog, however, only went from bad to worse. She rubbed against the posts of the corral or plunged impatiently into the brush, trying to shake off the gnats by flapping her dangling ears and swishing her short, hairy tail, thick at the base and coiled like a rattlesnake's.

So Fabiano decided to put an end to her. He went to look for his flintlock, polished it, cleaned it out with a bit of wadding, and went about loading it with care so the dog wouldn't suffer unduly.

Vitória shut herself up in the bedroom, dragging the children with her. They were frightened and, sensing misfortune, kept asking,

"Is the dog going to be hurt?"

They had seen the lead shot and the powder horn, and Fabiano's gestures worried them, causing them to suspect that the dog was in danger.

She was like a member of the family. There was hardly any difference to speak of between her and the boys. The three of them played together, rolling in the sand of the riverbed or in the loose manure, which, as it piled up, threatened to cover the goat pen.

The boys tried to push the latch and open the door, but Vitória dragged them over to the bed of tree branches, where she did her best to stop their ears, holding the head of the older between her thighs and putting her hands over the ears of the younger. Angry at the resistance they offered, she tried to hold them down by force, grumbling fiercely the while.

She too had a heavy heart, but she was resigned. Obviously Fabiano's decision was necessary and just. The poor dog!

Listening, she heard the noise of the shot being poured down the barrel of the gun, and the dull taps of the ramrod on the wadding. She sighed. The poor dog!

The boys began to yell and kick. Vitória had relaxed her muscles, and the bigger one was able to escape. She swore.

"Limb of Satan!"

In the struggle to get hold of the rebel again she really lost her temper. The little devil! She gave him a crack on the head, which he had plunged under the bedcovers and her flowered skirt.

Gradually her wrath diminished and, rocking the children, she began grumbling about the sick dog, muttering harsh names and expressions of contempt. The sight of the slobbering animal was enough to turn your stomach. It wasn't right for a mad dog to go running loose in the house. But then she realized she was being too severe. She thought it unlikely that the dog had gone mad and wished her husband had waited one more day to see whether it was really necessary to put the animal out of the way.

At that moment Fabiano was walking in the shed, snapping his fingers. Vitória drew in her neck and tried to cover her ears with her shoulders. As this was impossible, she raised her arms and, without letting go of her son, managed to cover a part of her head.

Fabiano walked through the lean-to, staring off toward the brauna trees and the gates, setting an invisible dog on invisible cattle.

"Sic 'em, sic 'em!"

Crossing the sitting room and the corridor, he came to the low kitchen window, from which, on examining the yard, he saw the dog scratching herself, rubbing the bare spots of her hide against the Jerusalem thorn. Fabiano raised the musket to his cheek. The dog eyed her master distrustfully and slipped sulkily around to the other side of the tree trunk, where she crouched with only her black eyes showing. Bothered by this maneuver on her part, Fabiano leaped out the window and stole along the corral fence to the corner post, where he again raised the arm to his cheek. As the animal was turned toward him and did not offer a very good target, he took a few more steps. On reaching the catingueira trees, he adjusted his aim and pulled the trigger. The load hit the dog in the hindquarters, putting one leg out of action. The dog began to yelp desperately.

Hearing the shot and the yelps, Vitória called upon the Virgin Mary, while the boys rolled on the bed, weeping aloud. Fabiano withdrew.

The dog fled in haste. She rounded the clay pit, went through the little garden to the left, passed close by the pinks and the pots of wormwood, slipped through a hole in the fence, and reached the yard, running on three legs. She had taken the direction of the shed but, fearing to meet Fabiano, she withdrew toward the goat pen. There she stopped for a moment, not knowing where to go, and then set off again, hopping along aimlessly.

In front of the oxcart her other back leg failed her, but, though bleeding profusely, she continued on her two front legs, dragging her hindquarters along as best she could. She wanted to retreat under the cart, but she was afraid of the wheel. She directed her course toward the jujube trees. There under one of the roots was a deep hole full of soft dirt in which she liked to wallow, covering herself with dust against the flies and gnats. When she would arise, with dry leaves and twigs sticking to her sores, she was a very different-looking animal.

She fell before reaching this distant refuge. She tried to get up, raising her head and stretching out her forelegs, but her body remained on its flank. In this twisted position she could scarcely move, though she scraped with her paws, digging her nails into the ground, pulling at the small pebbles. Finally she drooped and lay quiet beside the heap of stones where the boys threw dead snakes.

A horrible thirst burned her throat. She tried to look at her legs but couldn't make them out, for a mist veiled her sight. A desire came over her to bite Fabiano. She set up a yelp, but it was not really a yelp, just a faint howl that grew weaker and weaker until it was almost imperceptible.

Finding the sun dazzling, she managed to inch into a sliver of shade at the side of the stones.

She looked at herself again, worried. What was happening to her? The mist seemed ever thicker and closer.

A good smell of cavies drifted down to her from the hill, but it was faint and mingled with that of other creatures. The hill seemed to have grown far, far away. She wrinkled her muzzle, breathing the air slowly, desirous of climbing the slope and giving chase to the cavies, as they jumped and ran about in freedom.

She began to pant with difficulty, feigning a bark. She ran her tongue over her parched lips, but felt no relief. The smell was ever fainter: the cavies must certainly have fled.

She forgot them and once more had the desire to bite Fabiano, who appeared before her half-glazed eyes with a strange object in his hand. She didn't recognize it, but she began to tremble, sure that it held a disagreeable surprise for her. She made an effort to avoid it, pulling in her tail. Deciding it was out of harm's way, she closed her leaden eyes. She couldn't bite Fabiano; she had been born near him, in a bedroom, under a bed of tree branches, and her whole life had been spent in submission to him, barking to round up the cattle when the herdsman clapped his hands.

The unknown object continued to threaten her. She held her breath, covered her teeth, and peered out at her enemy from under her drooping eyelids. Thus she remained for some time, and then grew quiet. Fabiano and the dangerous thing had gone away.

With difficulty she opened her eyes. Now there was a great darkness. The sun must certainly have disappeared.

The bells of the goats tinkled down by the riverside; the strong smell of the goat pen spread over the surroundings.

The dog gave a start. What were those animals doing out at night? It was her duty to get up and lead them to the water hole. She dilated her nostrils, trying to make out the smell of the children. She was surprised by their absence.

She had forgotten Fabiano. A tragedy had occurred, but the dog did not see in it the cause of her present helplessness nor did she perceive that she was free of responsibilities. Anguish gripped at her small heart. She must mount guard over the goats. At that hour there should be a smell of jaguars along the riverbanks and in the distant tree clumps. Fortunately the boys were sleeping on the straw mat under the corner shelf, where Vitória kept her pipe.

A cold, misty, winter night enveloped the little creature. There was no sound or sign of life in the surroundings. The old rooster did not crow on his perch, nor did Fabiano snore in the bed of tree branches. These sounds were not in themselves of interest

91

to the dog, but when the rooster flapped his wings and Fabiano turned over, familiar emanations let her know of their presence. Now it seemed as if the ranch had been abandoned.

The dog took quick breaths, her mouth open, her jaw sagging, her tongue dangling, void of feeling. She didn't know what had happened. The explosion, the pain in her haunch, her difficult trip from the clay pit to the back of the yard faded out of her mind.

She was probably in the kitchen, in among the stones on which the cooking was done. Before going to bed, Vitória raked out the coals and ashes, swept the burnt area of the earthen floor with a broom, and left a fine place for a dog to take its rest. The heat kept fleas away and made the ground soft. And when she finally dozed off, a throng of cavies invaded the kitchen, running and leaping.

A shiver ran up the dog's body, from her belly to her chest. From her chest down, all was insensibility and forgetfulness, but the rest of her body quivered, and cactus spines penetrated the flesh that had been half eaten away by sickness.

The dog leaned her weary head on a stone. The stone was cold; Vitória must have let the fire go out very early.

The dog wanted to sleep. She would wake up happy, in a world full of cavies, and would lick the hands of Fabiano—a Fabiano grown to enormous proportions. The boys would roll on the ground with her in an enormous yard, would wallow with her in an enormous goat pen. The world would be full of cavies, fat and huge.

Accounts

In the division of stock at the year's end,
Fabiano received a fourth of the calves and a third of the kids,
but as he grew no feed, but merely sowed a few handfuls of
beans and corn on the river flat, living on what he bought at the
market, he disposed of the animals, never seeing his brand on a
calf or his mark on the ear of a kid.

If he could only put something aside for a few months, he
would be able to get his head up. Oh, he had made plans, but
that was all foolishness. Ground creepers were never meant to
climb. Once the beans had been eaten and the ears of corn
gnawed, there was no place to go but to the boss's cash drawer.
He would turn over the animals that had fallen to his lot for the
lowest of prices, grumbling and protesting in distress, trying to

make his meager resources yield as much as possible. Arguing, he would choke and bite his tongue. Dealing with anyone else he would not let himself be so shamelessly robbed, but, as he was afraid of being put off the ranch, he would give in. He would take the cash and listen to the advice that accompanied it. He should give thought to the future, be more careful. He would stand there with his mouth open, red-faced, his throat swelling. Suddenly he would burst out:

"Talk, talk! Money goes faster than a race horse, and people can't live without eating. Ground creepers were never meant to climb."

Little by little the boss's brand was put on Fabiano's stock, and when he had nothing left to sell, the backlander went into debt. When time came for the division, he was in the hole, and when accounts were settled he received a mere nothing.

This time, as on other occasions, Fabiano first made a deal regarding the stock, then thought better of the matter, and, leaving the transaction only half agreed upon, he went to consult with his wife. Vitória sent the boys to play in the clay pit, sat down in the kitchen, and concentrated, lining up different kinds of seeds on the ground, adding and subtracting. The next day Fabiano went back to town, but on closing the deal he noted that, as usual, Vitória's figuring differed from that of the boss. He protested, and received the usual explanation: the difference represented interest.

He refused to accept this answer. There must be some mistake. He was not very bright, that he knew. Anybody could see he was. But his wife had brains. Surely there was some mistake on the boss's paper. The mistake couldn't be found, and Fabiano lost his temper. Was he to take a beating like that his whole life long, giving up what belonged to him for nothing? Was that right? To work like a slave and never gain his freedom?

The boss became angry. He refused to hear such insolence. He thought it would be a good thing if the herdsman looked for another job.

At this point Fabiano got cold feet and began to back down. All right, all right. There was no need for a fuss. If he had said something wrong, he was sorry. He was ignorant; he had never had any learning. He knew his place; he wasn't the cheeky kind. He was just a half-breed. He wasn't going to get into any arguments with rich people. He wasn't bright, but he knew how to show people proper respect. His wife must just be mistaken, that was all. In fact her figuring had seemed strange to him. But since he didn't know how to read (he was just plain ignorant) he had believed his old lady. He was sorry and he wouldn't make a blunder like this again.

The boss calmed down and Fabiano backed out of the room, his hat dragging on the brick floor. Once outside the door he turned around, fastened the rowels on his spurs, and stumbled off, his untanned leather boots clumping on the ground like horses' hoofs.

He went to the corner, stopped, and caught his breath. They shouldn't treat him like that. He walked slowly toward the square. He made a wide circle around Inácio's tavern, and looked the other way. Since that trouble he had had he was afraid to go by there. He sat down on the sidewalk, took the money out of his pocket, and examined it, trying to guess how much he had been cheated. He couldn't say out loud it was robbery, but it was.

They gave him almost nothing for his stock and then on top of
that they invented interest. Interest! It was a dirty trick, that was
what it was.

"Robbery!"

He wasn't allowed to complain. Because he had protested, because he had thought the charge exorbitant, the boss had risen
up in fury and yelled at him. Why such a fuss?

He shook his head.

He remembered what had happened years ago, long before
the drought. One day when he was strapped for funds he turned
to the lean pig that refused to fatten in the stye and was being
saved for Christmas expenses. He had slaughtered it before its
time and had gone to sell it in town. But then some city official
had come with his receipt book and had crossed him up. Fabiano had pretended not to understand. He was just an ignorant
man from the country. Since the other fellow explained that in
order for him to sell the pig he would have to pay a tax, he tried
to convince him there was no pig there but just quarters of pork,
pieces of meat. The official had got angry and insulted him, and
Fabiano had cringed. All right, all right! Heaven forbid that he
get into any mix-up with the government. He had just thought
he could dispose of what was his. He didn't understand anything
about taxes.

"I'm just ignorant, you see."

He had supposed the hog was his. Now if the town government had some claim on it, that was that. He would go home and
eat the meat. Could he eat the meat? Could he or couldn't he?
The official had stamped in annoyance and Fabiano had made
excuses, his hat in his hand and his back bent.

"I don't want to get into any fight. I guess it will be better for me just to quit talking."

He took his leave, put the meat in his sack, and went to sell it secretly in another street. But the collector caught up with him, and he had not only a tax but a fine to lament. From that day on he stopped raising pigs. It was dangerous.

He looked at the bills neatly flattened out in his hand and at the silver and nickel coins; he sighed and bit his lips. He didn't even have the right to protest. He had drawn in his horns, for if he had not he would have had to leave the ranch and take to the road with his wife, his small sons, and his scanty belongings. And where would they go? Where? Did he have a place to take his wife and boys to? The devil he did!

He looked in all directions. The rooftops restricted his view but, beyond, the countryside stretched dry and hard. He remembered the painful trek he had made across it with his family, all of them in rags and famished. They had escaped, and this was a miracle in his eyes. He didn't even know how they had done it.

If he could move somewhere else he would shout from the housetops that he had been robbed. Resigned in appearance, he felt an immense hatred for something which was a combination of the dry countryside, the boss, the policemen, and the town officials. Really, everything was against him. He was used to it; his skin was hardened; but at times he got angry. No patience could hold out forever.

"The day comes when a man does something wild and that's the end of him."

Couldn't they see he was a man of flesh and blood? It was his duty to work for others, naturally. He knew his place. That was all right. He was born to this lot; it was nobody's fault that it was a hard one. What could he do? Could he change fate? If anyone were to tell him it was possible to better one's lot, he would be amazed. He had come into the world to break untamed horses, cure cattle ailments by prayer, and fix fences from winter to summer. It was fate. His father had lived like that, his grandfather too. Farther back than his grandfather, family did not exist for him. Cutting cactus, greasing rawhide whips—that was in his blood. He accepted the situation; he did not ask for more. If they only gave him what was coming to him, it was all right. But they didn't. He was a poor devil; like a dog, all he got was bones. Why then did rich people go and take part of the bones? It was sickening to think that important people would dirty their hands with things like that.

The bills were damp with sweat in the palm of his hand. He wanted to know just how much he had been done out of. The last time he had had an accounting with the boss it seemed to him he had come out better. He had a feeling of alarm. He had heard of interest and due dates, and this had made a rather painful impression on him. Whenever men with book learning used big words in dealing with him, he came out the loser. It startled him just to hear those words. Obviously they were just a cover for robbery.

But they sounded nice. Sometimes he memorized a few of them and introduced them into the conversation at the wrong moment. Then he forgot them. Why should a poor fellow like him go around talking like a rich man? Old Miss Terta now was one who had a terrible tongue for you. She talked almost as well as city folk. If he could talk like old Miss Terta, he would look for work at another ranch and would fix himself up. But he couldn't. In difficult moments he would stammer and get all mixed up like a little boy; he would scratch his elbows in vexation. This was why they skinned him, the scoundrels! They would take from a poor devil that didn't have a cent to his name. Couldn't they see it was wrong? What did they hope to gain by it? What?

He didn't grow pigs any more, and he would like to see that guy from the collector's office try to get a tax and a fine out of him. They took the shirt from his back and on top of that beat him and threw him in jail. Well, he wasn't going to work any longer; he was going to take a rest.

Perhaps he wasn't, though. Ceasing his monolog he counted and recounted mentally the money he had received. He balled it up with rage and thrust it into his pants pocket, which he buttoned. What a dirty business!

He got up and went to the door of a tavern, feeling like having a drink of rum. As there were a lot of people at the bar, however, he drew back. He didn't like to find himself in the midst of other people. He wasn't used to it. Sometimes he said something, without meaning to offend anyone, and they took it another way —and then there was trouble. It was dangerous to go into a tavern. The only living being who understood him was his wife. He didn't even have to talk to her; gestures were enough. Old Miss Terta now was a woman who could make herself understood like town folks. It was good for a body to be that way, to have the means of putting up a defense. He didn't. If he did, he wouldn't be in that state.

It was dangerous to go into the tavern. He felt like drinking half a pint of rum, but he remembered his last visit to Inácio's tavern. If he hadn't had the idea of drinking, that trouble wouldn't have happened. He couldn't even have a drink in peace. Well, he would go back home and sleep.

He went slinking along dejectedly, the rowels of his spurs making no noise. He wouldn't be able to sleep. In the bed of tree branches there was one with a knot in it, right in the middle. Only when he was dog-tired could a Christian get any rest on a thing as hard as that. He had to wear himself out on horseback or spend the whole day mending fences. Fagged out, completely limp, he would stretch out and snore away like a hog. But now he wouldn't be able to close his eyes. He would toss all night on the tree branches, mulling over the unfair way he had been treated. He would like to imagine what he was going to do in the future. He wasn't going to do anything! He would wear himself out working and would live in a house that belonged to someone else as long as they let him stay. Then he would have to take to the road and would die of hunger out on the dry brushland.

He took a piece of rope tobacco from his pocket and cut some off with his knife to make a cigarette. If he could at least recall some pleasant things life wouldn't be all bad.

He had left the street behind him. He raised his head and saw a star, then many stars. The figures of his enemies faded away. He thought of his wife, of his sons, of the dead dog. Poor thing! It was as if he had killed a member of the family.

The Policeman in Khaki

Fabiano started down the sun-baked path, overgrown with catingueira trees and clumps of bushes, that led to the dry pond. He was heavily laden. The haversack slung across his chest bulged and whips and cowbells dangled from one of his arms. His machete slapped against his leg.

He was studying the ground, as usual, trying to make out tracks. He recognized those of the gray mare and her foal—marks made by big hoofs and small ones. It must be the gray mare, for some whitish hairs were to be seen on the trunk of a mimosa tree. She had urinated on the sand and the urine had obliterated her tracks at that point, something which would not have happened in the case of a stallion.

Fabiano absent-mindedly noted these signs and others mingled with them, made by smaller animals. Bent over, he seemed to be sniffing at the earth. The deserted brush took on life for him as the beasts that had passed by returned before his little eyes.

He followed in the direction taken by the mare and had gone about two hundred yards when the halter that was slung over his shoulder caught on a bramble. He pulled it free, and taking out his machete began to hack away the thorns and the prickly pears that obstructed the path.

He had wrought havoc among them, covering the ground with spiny branches, when he stopped, hearing a noise in the twigs. Turning around, he came face to face with the policeman in khaki who a year earlier had thrown him in jail, where he had been beaten and had had to spend the night. Failing for a moment to recognize the figure that thus appeared before him, Fabiano started to bring his weapon down upon the stranger. The impulse lasted only for a second—no, less, a fraction of a second. Had it lasted longer, the khaki-clad figure would have lain kicking in the dust with his skull cleft open. As it was, the blade stopped short at the intruder's head, grazing his red cap. Only an equally strong, but contrary, second impulse had arrested a motion which could have resulted in homicide. At first the herdsman had understood nothing, save that he was in the presence of an enemy. Suddenly, however, he had noticed that it was a man, and, more important still, a representative of authority. He had stopped; his arm had hesitated, wavering from side to side.

The policeman, thin and puny, stood there trembling. Fabiano once more felt like raising his machete. He felt like it, but his muscles relaxed. Really, he didn't want to kill another Christian. He had acted instinctively, just as he avoided branches and thorns when breaking a horse. He wasn't conscious of his movements when in the saddle; something pushed him to the right or to the left. It was this something that had been going to make him split the khaki-wearer's head. If it had lasted a minute, Fabiano would have shown he was a man of real guts.

But it hadn't lasted. The certainty of danger had arisen, and he stood there, unable to make up his mind, breathing hard, true amazement showing on his sweat-covered face, his damp fingers providing but an unsure grip on the handle of his machete.

He was afraid, and he repeated to himself that he was in danger, but this seemed so absurd to him that he started to laugh. Afraid of that guy? He had never seen anyone tremble so. The dog! Didn't he act the bully in town? Wasn't he the man who trod on country folk's feet, the man who threw people into jail? The good-for-nothing scoundrel!

A feeling of irritation came over him. Why were that good-for-nothing's teeth chattering like a peccary's? Couldn't the guy see Fabiano was incapable of taking vengeance? He frowned. The thought of danger gradually disappeared. What danger? He didn't even need to take a machete to that wretch; his nails were all the weapon he needed. With a shake of the cowbells and whips he stuck his big hairy fist in the face of the policeman, who stepped back against a catingueira. Had the tree not been there, he would have fallen.

Fastening his bloodshot eyes on the man, Fabiano put his

machete back in its sheath. He could kill him just with his bare hands. He remembered the beating he had taken and the night he had spent in jail. Yes, sir. This guy was paid for mistreating folks who were only minding their own business. Was that right? Fabiano's face contracted, taking on a fearful appearance, uglier than an animal's snout. Well, was that right? To go bothering people who weren't harming anyone? Why? He choked. The wrinkles grew deeper on his forehead. His little blue eyes widened in a painful interrogation.

The policeman shrank back, hiding behind the tree. Fabiano dug his nails into his callused palms. He wanted to relive that first moment of blindness, but it was impossible. He repeated to himself that the weapon was unnecessary; he was sure that in any case he wouldn't be able to use it. He was just trying to deceive himself. For a moment the rage he experienced at feeling himself powerless was so great that he recuperated his energy and advanced upon his enemy.

His rage ceased, however, and the nails which were digging into his palms relaxed their grip. Fabiano stopped short and stood there as awkward and harmless-looking as a duck.

Clinging to the catingueira tree, the policeman showed only an arm, a leg, and a part of his face, but this strip of man began to grow in the herdsman's eyes. Obviously, the other part, that which was hidden, must be even bigger. Fabiano tried to rid himself of this absurd notion.

"What a crazy idea!"

A few minutes before he had nothing on his mind, but now he was in a cold sweat, plagued by unbearable recollections. He was a hot-tempered fellow, who easily flew off the handle. No, he was just a chap who let himself get peeved sometimes, and always had cause to regret it afterwards. That afternoon last year, for instance, if he hadn't lost his patience and made an insulting reference to the officer's mother, he wouldn't have spent a night in jail after first taking a beating. Two devils had fallen on him, whacking him with their knives, one on his back, the other on his chest, and he had dragged himself off, shivering like a wet hen. All because he had got angry and had come out with an ill-advised word. It was bad manners. But was he to blame? The hubbub had begun; the policeman had pushed a way for them through the market people who came crowding around. "Get a move on!"

Afterwards jail and a beating, all because of nothing at all. He, Fabiano, had been provoked. Had he, or hadn't he? A boot heel on his canvas sandal. He had lost patience and had come out with an insult. Now insulting a body's mother doesn't mean anything, because anyone can see no real harm is intended. It's just a meaningless bit of swearing. The fellow in khaki ought to have realized that. But he hadn't. He had got all hot under the collar, and had blown his whistle. And Fabiano had got the short end of the stick. "Get a move on!"

He took a step toward the tree. If he were to cry, "Get a move on!" now, what would the policeman do? He wouldn't move; he would stay glued to the trunk. The good-for-nothing! Anybody could insult his mother. But then— Fabiano stuck out his lower lip and snarled. That sickly creature in uniform put people in jail and beat them. He couldn't understand it. If he were a strong, healthy fellow, it would be all right. After all, it is no disgrace to take a beating from the government, and Fabiano could even feel proud in recalling the adventure. But that guy there! He gave a couple more snarls. Why did the government make use of people like that? Only if it were afraid to use decent folk. That pack was no good for anything but snapping at inoffensive people. Would he, Fabiano, act like that if he wore a uniform? Would he tread on the feet of honest working folk and give them beatings? He would not!

Slowly he drew near, made a turn, and found himself face to face with the policeman, who stood gaping, leaning against the trunk, his pistol and his dagger hanging uselessly at his side. Fabiano waited for him to move. He was a good-for-nothing, to be sure, but he wore a uniform and he certainly wasn't going to stand like that forever, his eyes bulging, his lips white, his teeth clacking together like a lacemaker's spools. He was going to stamp, to yell, to straighten his back, and to plant the heel of his boot on Fabiano's sandal. Fabiano wanted him to do that. The idea of having been insulted, jailed, and beaten by a weakling was unbearable. That cowardice reflected on him, made him seem more pitiful and contemptible than the policeman.

He lowered his head and scratched the reddish hairs on his chin. If the policeman didn't pull out his knife, if he didn't give a yell, he, Fabiano, was going to be most unhappy.

Should he bend before that trembling figure in khaki? He was thick-skinned; he had staying power and courage; he wanted to quarrel, to raise a row, and to come out of it with his head up. He remembered old fights over women that had taken place at dances, after he had had a few drinks of rum. Once, dagger in hand, he had sent the whole crowd running. That was when Vitória began to take a fancy to him. He had always been ill-tempered. Was he growing calmer with age? How old was he anyway? He didn't know, but he was certainly getting on, losing his strength. If he had a mirror, he would see wrinkles and white hair. A wreck! He hadn't felt the change, but he was wearing out.

Sweat dampened his horny hands. Well then, was he sweating with fear because of a good-for-nothing that hid and trembled? Wasn't that a terrible misfortune—the worst possible? Probably he would never get worked up again, but would spend the rest of his life like that, soft, without reacting to anything. How people change! Yes, he had changed. He was another person, far different from the Fabiano who had kicked up the dust in the dance halls. Now he was a Fabiano fit only to take a beating with the flat of a knife and to sleep in jail.

He turned his face aside and saw the machete dragging on the ground. That wasn't a machete; it was no good for anything.

The devil it wasn't!

Who said it wasn't?

It was a real machete all right; it flashed like lightning through the brambles. And it had been on the point of splitting open a scoundrel's head. It was sleeping now in its worn sheath; it was useless, but it had been a weapon. If things had lasted a second longer, the policeman would be dead. Fabiano imagined him lying there now, his legs spread apart, his eyes bulging with fear, a trickle of blood plastering his hair and forming a rivulet among the pebbles of the path. It would serve him right. He would drag him off into the brush and leave him to the vultures. And he would feel no remorse. He would sleep in peace with his wife, in their bed of tree branches. Afterwards he would yell at the boys, who needed to learn some manners. He was a man of guts, there was no doubt about that.

He straightened up and fixed his eyes upon those of the policeman, which dropped beneath his gaze. A man of guts. It was foolish to think he was going to go moping around the rest of his life. Was he worn out? He was not! But why should he wipe out that sickly creature that stood drooping there and seemed to ask to go down before him? Why should he make a mess of his life for a weakling in uniform who idled around the market and insulted poor folk? He wasn't going to make any such mistake; it wasn't worth it. He would save his strength.

He hesitated and scratched his head. There were a lot of characters like that, a lot that were both wicked and weak.

He drew back, perturbed. Seeing him thus humble and orderly, the policeman pricked up courage and advanced, stepping firmly, to ask directions. Fabiano took off his leather hat, bowed, and showed him the way.

"The law is the law."

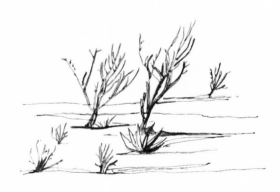

The Birds

The branches of the coral-bean tree down by the water hole were covered with birds of passage. This was a bad sign. In all probability the backland would soon be burnt up. The birds came in flocks; they roosted in the trees along the riverbank; they rested, they drank, and then, since there was nothing there for them to eat, they flew on toward the south. Fabiano and his wife, deeply worried, had visions of misfortunes to come. The sun sucked up the water from the ponds and those cursed birds drank up what was left, trying to kill the stock.

It was Vitória who said this. Fabiano grunted, wrinkled his brow, and found the expression exaggerated. The idea of birds killing oxen and goats! He looked at his wife distrustfully; he thought she was out of her mind. He went to sit on the bench under the shed, and from there he studied the sky, filled with a brightness that boded evil, its clear expanse broken only by the lines of passing birds. A feathered creature kill stock! Vitória must be crazy.

Fabiano stuck out his lower lip and wrinkled his sweaty brow still more deeply: it was impossible for him to understand what his wife meant. He couldn't get it. A little thing like a bird! As the matter seemed obscure to him he refrained from going into it any further. He went into the house, got his haversack, made himself a cigarette, struck the flint against the stone, and took a long drag. He looked in all directions and remained facing north for several minutes, scratching his chin.

"Awful! It's like the end of the world!"

He wouldn't stay there long. In the long-drawn-out silence all that could be heard was the flapping of wings.

What was it that Vitória had said? Her phrase came back to Fabiano's mind, and suddenly its meaning was apparent. The birds of passage drank the water. The stock went thirsty and died. Yes, the birds of passage did kill the cattle. That was right! Thinking the matter over you could see it was so, but Vitória had a complicated way of putting things. Now Fabiano saw what she meant. Forgetting imminent misfortune, he smiled, enchanted at Vitória's cleverness. A person like her was worth her weight in gold. She had ideas, she did! She had brains in her head. She could find a way out of difficult situations. There, hadn't she figured out that the birds of passage were killing the stock? And they were too! At that very hour the branches of the coral-bean tree down by the water hole, though stripped of blossoms and leaves, were a mass of feathers.

Desiring to see it up close he arose, slung his haversack across his chest, and went to get his leather hat and his flintlock. He stepped down from the shed, crossed the yard, and approached the slope, thinking of the dog. Poor thing! Those horrible-looking places had appeared around her mouth, her hair had dropped out, and he had had to kill her. Had he done right? He had never thought about that before. The dog was sick. Could he risk her biting the children? Could he? It was madness to expose the boys to rabies. Poor dog! He shook his head to get her out of his mind. It was that devilish flintlock that brought the image of the little dog back to him. Yes, it was certainly the flintlock. He turned his face away as he passed the stones at the end of the yard where they had found the dog, cold and stiff, her eyes pecked out by the vultures.

Taking longer steps he went down the slope and walked across the river flat toward the water hole. There was a wild flapping of wings over the pool of dark water. The branches of the coral-bean tree couldn't even be seen. What a flock of pests! When they came in from the backland they made an end of everything. The stock was going to waste away, and even the thorns would dry up.

He sighed. What was he to do? Flee once more, settle some place else, begin life all over again. He raised his gun and pulled the trigger without even aiming. Five or six birds fell to the ground. The rest took flight and the dry branches appeared in all their nakedness. Little by little they were covered again. There was no end to it.

Fabiano sat down dispiritedly at the edge of the water hole. Slowly he loaded the flintlock with bird shot, but did not use any wadding, so the load would spread and hit many enemies. There was a new report and new birds fell, but this gave Fabiano no pleasure. He had food there for two or three days; if he had enough munition he would have food for weeks and months.

He examined the powder horn and the leather shot holder; he thought of the trip and shuddered. He tried to deceive himself into thinking it wouldn't come about if he didn't provoke it by evil thoughts. He relit his cigarette and sought to distract himself by talking in a low voice. Old Miss Terta was a person who knew a lot about that part of the country. What could be the state of his accounts with the boss? That was something he could never figure out. That business of interest swallowed up everything, and on top of it all the boss acted as if he were doing a favor. Then there was that policeman in khaki—

Fabiano closed his fists and punched himself in the thigh for his bad luck. The devil! There he was, trying to forget one misfortune, and others came crowding upon him. He didn't want to think either of the boss or of the policeman in khaki. But to his despair they insisted on coming to his mind, and he tightened up like a rattlesnake coiling in anger. He was unlucky, the unluckiest fellow in the world. He ought to have struck the policeman in khaki that afternoon; he ought to have carved him up with his machete. But like a good-for-nothing country lout he had pulled in his horns and had showed the policeman the way. He rubbed his sweaty, wrinkled brow. Why bring his shame back to mind, though? He was just a poor devil. But was he determined to go on living like that forever? Worthless and weak, that was what he was. If he hadn't been so timid he would have joined a gang of bandits and would have gone around wreaking destruction. Eventually he would get shot in ambush, or would spend his old age serving out a sentence in jail. This was better, though, than dying by the roadside in the broiling heat, his wife and boys dying too. He ought to have cut the policeman's throat, taking his own good time about doing it. They could put him in jail then, but he would be respected—yes, respected, as a man of guts. The way he was now, nobody could respect him. He wasn't a man; he wasn't anything. He had suffered a beating and had not taken revenge.

"Fabiano, my boy, get your chin up! Get some self-respect! Kill the policeman in khaki! Policemen in khaki are a pack of scoundrels that ought to be put out of the way. Kill the policeman and the people he gets his orders from!"

He began to pant and be thirsty as a result of the energy wasted in his wild gesticulations. Sweat ran down over his red, sunburned face and darkened his ruddy beard. He came down from the bank and bent over the edge of the hole, lapping the brackish water from his cupped hands. A throng of startled birds of passage took flight. Fabiano got up with a flash of indignation in his eyes.

"Dirty, low-down—"

His anger was once again turned against the birds. Sitting back down on the bank, he fired many times into the branches of the coral-bean tree, leaving the ground covered with dead bodies. They would be salted and hung up on a line to dry. He intended to use them for food on the coming journey. He should spend the rest of his money on powder and shot and put in a day there at

the water hole, then take to the road. Would he have to move? Although he knew perfectly well he would, he clung to frail hopes. Perhaps the drought wouldn't come; perhaps it would rain.

It was those cursed birds that frightened him. He tried to forget them. But how could he forget them if they were right there, flying about his head, hopping around on the mud, perching on the branches, lying scattered in death on the ground? Were it not for them, the drought would not exist. At least it would not exist just then. It would come later and last a shorter time. As things were, it was beginning now; Fabiano could feel it already. It was just as if it had arrived; he was already suffering the hunger, thirst, and endless fatigue of the trek. A few days earlier he had been calmly making whips and mending fences. Suddenly there was a dark line across the sky, then other lines, thousands of lines uniting to form clouds, and the fearful noise of wings,

heralding destruction. He had already suspected something when he saw the springs diminishing, and he had looked with distrust at the whiteness of the long mornings and the sinister redness of the afternoons. Now his suspicions were confirmed.

"Miserable wretches!"

Those cursed birds were the cause of the drought. If he could kill them the drought would be choked off. He moved feverishly, loading the flintlock with fury. His thick, hairy hands, full of blotches and skinned spots, trembled as they moved the ramrod up and down.

"Pests!"

But it was impossible to put an end to that plague. He looked about the countryside and found himself completely isolated. Alone in a world of feathers, full of birds that were going to eat him up. He thought of his wife and sighed. Poor Vitória would again have to carry the tin trunk across the wasteland. It was hard for a woman with her brains to go tramping over the scorched earth, bruising her feet on the stones. The birds of passage were killing the stock. How had Vitória hit on that idea? It was hard. He, Fabiano, no matter how he might rack his brains, would never come out with an expression like that. Vitória knew how to figure accounts right; she sat down in the kitchen, consulted piles of different kinds of seeds, representing coins of varying value. And she came out right. The boss's accounts were different, drawn up in ink, against the herdsman, but Fabiano knew that they were wrong and that the boss was trying to cheat him. He did cheat him. But what could he do about it? Fabiano, a luckless half-breed, slept in jail and was beaten. Could he react? He could not. He was just a half-breed.

But Vitória's accounts must be right. Poor Vitória. She would never be able to stretch her bones in a real bed, the only thing she truly wanted. Didn't other people sleep in beds? Fearing to wound her feelings, Fabiano would agree with her, though it was just a dream. They couldn't sleep like Christians. And now they were going to be eaten up by the birds of passage.

He got down from the bank, slowly picked up the dead birds, filling his haversack to overflowing with them, and gradually withdrew. He, Vitória, and the two boys would eat the birds.

If the dog were still alive, she would have a feast. Why did he feel such a stab at his heart? The poor dog! He had had to kill her, because she was sick. Then he had gone back to the whips, the fences, and the boss's mixed-up accounts. He walked up the slope and approached the jujubes. At the root of one of them the poor dog loved to wallow, covering herself with twigs and dry leaves. Fabiano sighed. He felt a tremendous weight in his chest. Had he been wrong? He looked at the burnt plain, the hill where the cavies hopped about, and he swore to the catingueira trees and the stones that the animal had rabies and threatened the children. That was why he had killed her. And he had given the matter no further thought at the time.

Here Fabiano's thoughts became mixed up. The idea of the dog mingled with that of the birds of passage, which he failed to distinguish from the drought. He, his wife, and the two boys would be eaten up. Vitória was right; she was smart and saw things a long way off. Fabiano's eyes widened; he wanted to go on admiring her, but his heart was heavy. It felt as big as a bullfrog; it was full of thoughts of the dog. The poor thing, thin and stiff, her eyes pecked out by the vultures!

Passing in front of the jujubes, Fabiano walked more quickly. How could he tell whether the dog's spirit wasn't haunting the place?

Fear was in his soul as he reached the house. It was dusk, and at that hour he always felt a vague terror. He had been discouraged and dejected of late because misfortunes had been many. He would have to consult with Vitória about the trip, get rid of the birds he had shot, explain himself, convince himself he had not done wrong in killing the dog. They would have to abandon the accursed place. Vitória would think just as he did.

Flight

Life on the ranch had become difficult. Vitória crossed herself trembling, she told her beads, her wrinkled lips moved in desperate prayers. Slumped on the bench in the shed, Fabiano gazed at the yellow brushland where dry leaves, blown about by the swirling winds, turned to dust, leaving only twisted, scorched, black branches. The last birds of passage had disappeared from the azure sky. Little by little the stock wasted away, devoured by ticks. Still Fabiano resisted, begging God for a miracle.

When he saw the ranch lifeless, however, he realized all was lost and made arrangements for the trek with his wife. He slaughtered the murrain-infected calf they still owned, salted the meat, and set off with his family, without taking leave of the boss. He could never settle that preposterous debt. All he could do was take to the road, like a fugitive slave.

They left before daybreak. Vitória stuck her arm through a hole in the wall and closed the front-door latch. They crossed the yard, leaving behind them in the darkness the goat pen and the corral—now empty and with their gates hanging open—the rotting oxcart, and the two jujubes. On passing by the pile of stones on which the boys used to throw dead snakes, Vitória remembered the dog and wept, but no one could see her tears in the dark.

They went down the slope, crossed the dry riverbed, and set

out for the south. In the cool of the predawn they walked in silence for quite a distance, four shadows on the narrow road covered with small pebbles—the two boys in front, carrying bundles of clothing, Vitória with the painted tin trunk and the water gourd, Fabiano bringing up the rear with his machete and his dagger, the drinking gourd hanging from a cord tied to his waist, his haversack slung across his chest, his flintlock over one shoulder and the sack of provisions over the other. They covered a good three leagues before the first light of day appeared.

They made a halt. Fabiano put part of his burden on the ground and looked at the sky, shading his eyes with his hands. He had dragged himself there, unsure whether it was really a move they were making. He had hung back and had reproved the boys who had gone on ahead, counseling them to save their strength. The truth was that he didn't want to go away from the ranch. The trek seemed a bungle to him; he didn't really believe in it. He had prepared for it, slowly; he had put it off and had again prepared for it; and he had finally resolved to leave only when everything was definitely lost. Could he go on living in a cemetery? Nothing bound him to that hard earth; he could find some place less dry to be buried. That was what Fabiano said as he thought of other things—the goat pen and the corral, whose fences needed mending; the horse the boss had given him to use and that had proved a good companion; the sorrel mare; the catingueira trees; the pots of wormwood; the stones on which they did the cooking; the bed of tree branches. His feet lost all enthusiasm; his sandals were silent in the darkness. Would he have to abandon everything? His sandals began to squeak again on the pebble-covered road. Fabiano studied the sky, where a line of light brightened the horizon. He refused to accept reality. His heart filled with misgiving, he sought to make out something different from the reddishness which all the others saw. His thick hands trembled under the curved brim of his hat as they protected his eyes against the brightness.

He dropped his arms dispiritedly.

"It's all over."

Even before looking at the sky he knew it was black in one direction and blood red in the other and that it was going to turn bright blue. He shuddered as if he had discovered something profoundly evil.

Ever since the appearance of the birds of passage he had been uneasy. He had worked long hours, to make sure he would sleep, but in the midst of his labor a shiver would run down his spine, and at night he would awaken in agony and curl up in a corner of the bed of tree branches, where, devoured by fleas, he would conjure up visions of coming misfortunes.

The light increased and spread over the range. Only then did the trek really begin. Fabiano picked up the flintlock and the bag of provisions, gave a look at his wife and sons, and with a hoarse cry ordered them to set off.

They walked rapidly, as if someone were goading them on, Fabiano's sandals all but treading on the boys' heels. The herdsman had to get away from that hostile land, where mandacarus and other cactus covered the range, where nothing but thorns were to be seen on every side. He couldn't get the dog out of his mind; the recollection pricked unbearably at his conscience.

The boys ran along. Vitória glanced down at her rosary of blue and white beads, tucked in her bosom; at this movement of her head the painted tin trunk all but fell. She straightened up, adjusted the trunk's position, and moved her lips in a prayer. God our Savior would protect innocent sufferers. Vitória had a moment of weakness as an immense tenderness filled her heart. Her courage soon returned, however, and she tried to rid herself of sad thoughts by talking with her husband in monosyllables. Though she had a good tongue, a lump in her throat now kept her from expressing her thoughts. She felt small and alone in the midst of that solitude; she needed someone for support, someone to give her courage. She longed for a sound of some sort, but no voice of bird, rustle of leaf, or whisper of wind broke the deathlike silence of the morning. The red band of the horizon had disappeared, melting into the blue which filled the sky.

Vitória simply had to talk. If she kept silence she would be like a cactus plant, drying up and dying. She wanted to deceive herself, to cry out that she was strong and that all this—the frightful heat, the trees that were no more than twisted branches, the motionlessness and silence of the range—meant nothing. She drew apace with Fabiano. Deriving comfort for herself from that which she offered him, she forgot nearby objects, the thorns, the birds of passage, and the vultures looking for carrion. She spoke of the past, confusing it with the future. Couldn't they go back to being what they had been?

Fabiano hesitated, scratched his beard, and mumbled as he always did when people addressed him in terms he did not understand. He was glad though that Vitória had started a conversation. He was completely discouraged; the bag of provisions and the haversack were beginning to be unbearably heavy. Vitória put her question; Fabiano went a good half league meditating without understanding. At first he was inclined to answer that of course they were what they had been; then he decided they had changed: they were older and less strong. To put it right, they were different. Vitória insisted. Wouldn't it be good to live again as they had lived, far away? Fabiano shook his head in vacillation. Perhaps, perhaps not. They had a long whispered conversation, broken off at intervals, full of misunderstandings and repetitions. To live as they had lived in a little house sheltered by Tomás' mill. They discussed the matter and ended by recognizing that it wouldn't be worth while, as they would always be on tenterhooks, thinking of drought.

They were now on their way to inhabited areas. They should find a place to live there. They couldn't always go wandering like gypsies. The herdsman's spirit was clouded at the thought that he was going toward lands where perhaps there was no stock to care for. Vitória tried to cheer him by saying that he could take up other occupations. Fabiano trembled, turned, and gazed in the direction of the abandoned ranch. He remembered the cattle with their sores, but then he wiped the thought from his mind. What was he doing looking back? The animals were dead. He closed his eyes tightly to hold back tears as a great homesickness filled his heart. A moment later, though, images he could not bear to recall came to his mind: the boss, the policeman in khaki, the dog stiff in death by the stones at the end of the yard.

The boys disappeared around a curve in the road. Fabiano moved to catch up with them. Advantage had to be taken of their eagerness; they must be allowed to go as they pleased. Vitória accompanied him and soon they overtook the children. On round-ing the curve, Fabiano felt himself a little farther from the place they had lived for a few years; the figures of the boss, the policeman in khaki, and the dog faded from his thoughts.

The conversation resumed. Fabiano was now a bit more optimistic. He adjusted the position of the sack of provisions; he examined his wife's full face and thick legs approvingly. He felt like smoking, but he was holding the mouth of the sack and the butt of the flintlock and could not satisfy his desire. He was afraid of giving up, of not continuing the journey. He went on chattering, tossing his head to keep off a cloud which, if viewed closely, would be seen to conceal the boss, the policeman in khaki, and the dog. His callused feet, hard as hoofs, shod with new sandals, would hold out for months. Or would they? Vitória thought they would. Fabiano was grateful for her opinion and praised her sturdy legs, her broad hips, and her full breasts. Vitória's cheeks reddened, and Fabiano repeated his compliment with enthusiasm. What he had said was right: she was big and strong and could walk a long way. Vitória laughed and lowered her eyes. He was exaggerating. She would soon be thin and slack-breasted. But she would put on weight again. And perhaps the place where they were going would be better than the ones where they had been before. Fabiano stuck out his lower lip doubtfully. Vitória combated his doubt. Why couldn't they live like other people, have a bed like Tomás the miller's? Fabiano scratched his head; there came her crazy ideas again! Vitória insisted, dominating him. Why should they always be out of luck; why should they always be fleeing off to the wilds, like animals? There were wonderful things to be seen in the world. Surely they couldn't go on living in hiding like beasts. Fabiano agreed.

"The world is a big place."

In reality their world was a very small one, but they declared it was big and walked on, half trusting, half uneasy. They looked at the children, who were staring at the distant hills, where they divined mysterious beings.

"What do you suppose they're thinking of?" Vitória murmured.

Fabiano wondered at the question and mumbled an objection. Boys are small fry; they don't think. But Vitória repeated her question, and her husband wasn't so sure. She must be right. She was always right. Now she wanted to know what the boys were going to do when they grew up.

"Herd cattle," was Fabiano's opinion.

Vitória made a face of disgust, shaking her head in disagreement, at the risk of causing the tin trunk to fall. Our Lady save them from such misfortune! Herd cattle! What an idea! They were going to a far country, where they would forget the brushland with its hills and hollows, its pebbles, its dry rivers, thorns, vultures, dying cattle, and dying people. They would never come back; they would resist the homesickness that attacks backlanders in green country. Were they to die of sadness for lack of thorns? They would settle down far away and would take on new ways.

Fabiano listened to his wife's dreaming in fascination; his muscles relaxed and the bag of provisions slipped from his shoulder. He straightened up and gave a yank at his load. Vitória's conversation had helped a lot; they had walked for leagues and scarcely noticed it. Suddenly they felt weak. It must be hunger. Fabiano raised his head and squinted out under the black, burnt brim of his leather hat. It was around noon. Lowering his half-blinded eyes, he sought to make out a sign of shade or water on the plain. He felt as if he had a hole in his stomach. He straightened the sack again and, so as to keep it from slipping, he walked leaning to one side, one shoulder higher than the other. Vitória's optimism no longer made any impression on him. She still clung to dreams, poor thing. Making plans like that when she was bending under the weight of the trunk and the water gourd that pushed her neck down into her shoulders!

They sought rest under the bare branches of a quixaba tree. They chewed on some handfuls of manioc flour and bits of dry meat and had a few sips of water from the gourd. On Fabiano's brow the sweat was drying, mingling with the dust which filled the deep wrinkles, or soaking into the hat strap. His dizziness had disappeared; his stomach was calm. When they set out again, Vitória's spine would no longer bend under the weight of the water gourd. Instinctively his eyes swept over their desolate surroundings in search of signs of water. A cold chill ran over him. His yellow teeth showed in a childish grin. How could he be cold with such heat? For a moment he stood there like a simpleton, looking at his sons, his wife, and the heavy baggage. The older boy was picking a bone with gusto. Fabiano remembered the dog, and another shiver ran down his spine. His foolish smile faded.

If they found water near at hand, they would drink a lot and go on their way full, dragging their feet. So said Fabiano to Vitória, pointing out a low-lying place in the terrain. It was a water hole, wasn't it? Vitória stuck out her lip in indecision, and Fabiano now affirmed what he had first asked. Didn't he know that country? Was he talking nonsense? If his wife had agreed with him, Fabiano's assurance would have waned, since he lacked conviction, but since she expressed doubt Fabiano worked himself up, trying to put courage into her. He invented the water hole and described it, lying without realizing he was lying. Then Vitória became excited and transmitted hope to him. They were traveling through country with which they were acquainted. What was Fabiano's job? Looking after stock, exploring the country from horseback. And he explored everything. Beyond the distant hills was another world, one to be feared, but here on the plain he knew plants, animals, holes, and stones by heart.

The boys stretched out and went to sleep. Vitória asked her companion for the tinder and lit her pipe. Fabiano made himself a cigarette. For the time being they were at peace. The possibility of a water hole had become a reality. They went back to making plans in a low voice as the smoke from the cigarette mingled with that of the pipe. Fabiano insisted on his topographical knowledge and spoke of the horse the boss had given him to use. It was surely going to die. Such a fine animal! If it had come with them, it would have carried their belongings. For a while it would have lived on dry leaves, but beyond the hills it would have found green things to eat. Unfortunately, it belonged to the ranch owner, and it was wasting away with no one to give it feed. His friend was going to die, full of sores and with spavins, in a fence corner, seeing the vultures come hopping unsteadily, their bills threatening his eyes. The thought of the frightful birds with their hooked beaks menacing the eyes of living creatures filled Fabiano with horror. If they would be patient they could eat the carrion at ease. But they weren't patient, those voracious devils that flew in circles up there overhead.

"Devils!"

They were always flying around. You couldn't figure where so many vultures came from.

"Devils!"

He looked at the moving shadows that covered the range. Perhaps they were circling around the poor horse, lying faint in a fence corner. Fabiano's eyes grew damp. The poor horse. It was thin, it had lost its hair, it was hungry and turned on him big, round eyes like those of people.

"Devils!"

What angered Fabiano was the habit the wretches had of pecking at the eyes of creatures that could no longer defend themselves. He arose with a start, as if the birds had come down from the blue sky and were close at hand, flying in ever smaller circles around his body and those of Vitória and the boys.

Vitória noted the uneasiness in his tortured face and got up too. She awakened her sons and packed the household belongings. Fabiano took up his burden. Vitória untied the thong from his belt and took the gourd from it. She placed it upside down on a pad of rags on the older boy's head, then set a bundle on top. Fabiano approved of the arrangement, smiling and forgetting the horse and the vultures. Yes, sir! What a woman! That way his load would be lighter and the youngster would have a sunshade. The weight of the gourd was insignificant, but Fabiano felt light and walked firmly in the direction of the water hole. They would arrive there before night; they would drink, rest, and continue their journey by moonlight. All this was dubious, but it was taking on credibility. And the conversation resumed as the sun sank in the west.

"I've had harder nuts to crack," Fabiano declared, defying the sky, the thorns, and the vultures.

"You think so?" Vitória murmured, not so much questioning as confirming what he said.

Little by little a new life, as yet indistinct, took hold of their imagination. They would settle on a small farm, though this seemed hard to Fabiano, who had grown up running loose in the brush. They would cultivate a piece of ground. Afterwards they would move to the city and the boys would go to school. They would be different from their parents. Vitória waxed enthusiastic. Fabiano laughed; he wanted to rub his hands together, but they were holding the mouth of the sack and the butt of the flintlock.

He did not feel the weight of the gun or the sack, or the small pebbles that had got into his sandals. Neither did he note the stench of carrion that hung over the road. He was under the spell of Vitória's words. They would go forward; they would come to an unknown land. Fabiano was happy; he believed in that land because he didn't know what it was like or where it was. Docilely he repeated Vitória's words—words which she murmured because she had confidence in him. They trudged southward, enveloped in their dream.

A big city, full of strong people. The boys at school, learning difficult but necessary things. The two of them old, ending their lives like a pair of useless dogs—like the dog they once had.

But what were they going to do? They hung back, fearful. They were on their way to an unknown land, a land of city ways. They would become its prisoners.

And to the city from the backland would come ever more and more of its sons, a never-ending stream of strong, strapping brutes like Fabiano, Vitória, and the two boys.

Other Texas Pan American paperbacks